Shopkeeper's Widow

Izzy James

The Shopkeeper's Widow
COPYRIGHT 2020 by Elizabeth C. Hull

Cover Art by *Nicola Martinez*

White Rose Publishing, a division of Pelican Ventures, LLC
www.pelicanbookgroup.com PO Box 1738 *Aztec, NM * 87410
White Rose Publishing Circle and Rosebud logo is a trademark of Pelican Ventures, LLC

Publishing History
First White Rose Edition, 2020
Electronic Edition ISBN 978-1-5223-0301-5
Paperback Edition ISBN 9781522303732
Published in the United States of America

Dedication

This one is for Bean, whose encouragement came when
I needed it.
I love ya, man.
Iz

Prologue

March 1767
Archer Hall, Northumberland County, Virginia

"Dandelion." Field Archer twisted the stem of the blow-ball between his fingers. "From the French, *dent de lion*. Literally, 'lion's tooth.'"

Delany Button hopped up from where she'd sat making a daisy chain of dandelions to face him in the field dotted with yellow blooms. Her breath caught in her throat when he looked into her eyes. This was how it would be when she walked in holding his arm following the minister on her wedding day.

She would wear a gown of silver silk. He wouldn't be able to take his eyes off her then. Papa said she had Mama's coloring and that silver was just the thing for her auburn hair and gray eyes. Fifteen was still a bit young for marriage, but she'd heard of a girl, just last week, who married at fourteen.

He blew the seed-ball.

She breathed in the warmth of his breath. Filaments landed on her eyelashes causing her to snap her eyes shut. She drifted them open to see him turn and blow the rest into the field around them.

"Ingenious," he said. "The seeds fly on the wind.

They land, take root in the soil..." Field continued to expound on the virtues of dandelions as they walked toward the house. He loved farming. He could talk for hours about the plants they grew and why they grew them.

And when she came for her biannual visits, Delany was always glad to listen. She hadn't heard the rest of today's lesson for the vision of what it would be like to be in his arms.

Perhaps tonight, at the party, she would find out. Mrs. Archer said there would be dancing and that she might attend. Field's sister, Amity, had loaned her a gown of real pink silk.

~*~

The transformed dining room gleamed. Tables had been removed, chairs lined the walls. Dozens of candles filled the room with the soft light of romance. Cool breezes from the Potomac salted the magnolia-spiced air, sailing in through large open windows on both ends of the hall, mingling with the scent of freshly polished wooden floors.

Delany shivered. A dance. Real silk. Dreams really did come true.

Dancers assembled in the center eager to begin.

Others chatted merrily in groups.

Across the room, Field stood with his friend, Simon Morgan, smiling and laughing. Belonging.

Sweaty palms skidded down the cool pink silk when she attempted to smooth her skirts. She could almost forget she was indentured. Her father had promised that these few years would set them up for life. Once their time was finished, he would be a gentleman farmer, and she would be his daughter. Three whole years before she was free.

Would Field want to marry her then?

"Come on, silly." Amity pulled her by the elbow into the room. The two skirted the dancers to find empty chairs on the wall near the end of the line. Amity took the seat that gave her the best view of Simon Morgan which left Delany with her back to Field.

The band finished; the dancers dispersed to the sidelines. New couples formed and headed back toward the center.

"I see your sister and her friend are free." Simon's low voice carried under the giggling din.

Delany's heart skipped in anticipation.

Amity's smile radiated expectation.

"You go right ahead," Field rejoined. "Her 'friend,' as you call her, is just a servant. She's indentured to the merchant, Fleet, from Norfolk. I assume Mama allowed her to come for her improvement."

Delany's stomach clenched.

Within an instant, Simon Morgan stood in front of Amity, offering her his hand. Dizzy and frozen in place, Delany watched Amity place her hand in his and glide toward the dancers as the chords of the next dance began. She took deep breath and rose from her seat. She took careful steps not to disturb any of the real guests and made her way softly to her room.

1

Circular Letter from the Earl of Dartmouth to the Governours of the Colonies

Whitehall, October 19, 1774

Sir:

His Majesty having thought fit by his Order in Council this day to prohibit the exportation from Great Britain of Gunpowder, or any sort of Arms or Ammunition, I herewith enclose to you a copy of the order; and it is His Majesty's command that you do take the most effectual measures for arresting, detaining, and securing any Gunpowder, or any sort of Arms or Ammunition which may be attempted to be imported into the Province under your Government, unless the master of the ship having such Military Stores on board shall produce a license from his Majesty or the Privy Council for the exportation of the same from some of the Ports of this Kingdom.

I am, Sir, your most obedient humble servant,

DARTMOUTH

30 September 1775
Borough of Norfolk, Virginia

With a startled swipe of her arm, Delany Fleet brushed Noah's animals to the floor. Still grasping the tiny wooden giraffe from the set she'd been arranging, she hurried toward the door of her shop and the sound of the drum.

Outside, fifteen British soldiers marched up the narrow, mud-caked street. Bayonets glinted in the early afternoon sun. Redcoats crisp against white lapels. Black boots marched in cadence with the drum.

Her heart thumped with the beat. Behind them, in the harbor, the fourteen-gun sloop-of-war, *Otter*, leveled its barrels at the borough.

People streamed out of their shops and houses to witness the spectacle.

Delany had grown accustomed to the sight of soldiers making a nuisance of themselves around Norfolk, but this formal display of British military strength took her breath away. It was Lord Dunmore's latest ploy to control the "rebellious" Virginia colony. If only all this unrest would go away. She'd worked too hard to lose everything in a game of politics in which she had no part.

The soldiers marched two abreast, a wall of hewed stone. The men towered above her own sixty-inch height, faces wiped of all expression.

Their power stirred in her rebellious emotions she thought dead with her late husband, Tom. The spell broke when her nephew, Ben, arrived at her side. She pulled him close. At thirteen, Ben itched to join the militia. This display wouldn't help matters. Forgetting the open shop, she and Ben followed the crowd as the column made a turn onto Main Street and arrived at the *Virginia Gazette*.

The drum stopped.

The wall broke into parts and entered the small building. The sounds of wood scraping and splintering, men yelling, and boxes crashing to the floor burst into the street. The crowd, with backward glances at the wharf, resisted only in murmurs.

Delany stood mesmerized. A white-hot spot of indignation began to build in the very core of her being. *How would John feed his family? Who would be next?*

"The shop!" Delany's heart nearly stopped when she remembered the unlocked door, "Ben, run. I left the shop open." People from all over the world washed up on Norfolk's shores. The neighbors wouldn't rob her, but who knew all their neighbors in a seaport?

Ben took off running.

Short, scruffy Josiah Dean beat the drum to assemble and call the militia to action.

Delany searched the crowd for signs of the militia. No one answered the call. *Where were they?*

A hundred people watched as the wall reformed. This time they did not march as their arms were full of John's property: press types, ink pots, paper, and components of the press itself. Frank Cumming and Joseph Smith, bookbinder and journeyman, stumbled in their midst when pushed and prodded by armed guards.

Delany headed back toward her shop and Ben, continuously searching the crowd for any sign of resistance.

Josiah's drum continued to call.

The soldiers climbed into the skiff waiting to take them back to the ship. Once aboard, they shouted huzzah three times and rowed away from the borough.

A shiver of anger shook Delany as she re-entered Fleet's Toy and Curiosities Shop. A quick glance at the shelves and windows assured her of no disturbance save her own scattering of Noah's animals.

"Did the militia come?" Ben pressed against the window glass as the dispersing crowd passed by.

"No. Frightened by the *Otter*'s guns, no doubt. That was Josiah Dean you heard on the drum."

"They better not come here." He mimicked shooting his rifle. "I'll kill them."

"No. You. Won't. And if you keep talking like that, I'll have to take you back to your papa."

His arms flopped down to his sides. "Aunt Delany, we can't just let them come in here." Ben looked around the shop. "Papa would want me to defend you."

"Benjamin Fleet." She gave him the stern look that always shut him up. "Enough."

He turned back to the window.

"Have you finished your sums?"

Without answering, he left the window and headed to his desk in the back room.

Swallowing her anger, she bent down to pick up

Noah's animals. Inspecting each for damage, she replaced them gently on the display shelf. It had taken her days to persuade Ann Archer to let her sell the toys. She smiled at the memory of the gentle lady.

This was her shop. Her future depended on the income she earned from the toys and other items she carefully chose to stock. Soon, she would have enough saved to leave Norfolk's muddy, congested streets for the country. If only Lord Dunmore would hold off for another year. The house on her new farm in Northumberland County would be finished, and she would be safe. Her own land. A home that was truly her own, where she'd never been a servant. A place that no one could take from her. A place from which no one could take her. Now that was something that would make Papa proud.

The door opened, and Sarah Harrison entered. A few minutes later, Nanny Settle arrived, followed by Lucy Spitler. All three members of the prayer group assembled at the table in the back room. Delany picked up her Bible from under the counter and joined them.

Once seated, with Ben stationed by the doorway, Sarah opened with a short prayer and read from Matthew chapter eighteen. Afterward each had an opportunity to pray. Nanny Settle prayed for John Holt's family. Lucy Spitler prayed for Norfolk and the colony. Sarah Harrison prayed for the soldiers. Ben prayed for the militia to be "brave and fight like men." Silence stretched thin as they waited for Delany.

Sarah was right; they needed to pray for both sides. It was never clear to her which side the Lord was on, and as He was the Lord of individuals, she had resolved to keep as neutral as possible. That had changed yesterday when a musket had been fired into Norfolk from another of Lord Dunmore's four sloops-of-war, the *King Fisher*. Lord Dunmore had declared it an accident.

Today was not an accident.

Delany seethed.

"Delany, do you wish to pray?" Sarah prompted.

"No," Delany whispered.

Sarah ended with a final prayer for wisdom.

Ben hopped up and bolted out the back door with the final "Amen".

Three women, their eyes filled with concern, faced her.

"Delany, are you feeling well?" Sarah asked.

"I am so angry I don't know how to pray." Delany stood. "How dare they come here and steal John's press?"

"I've been on edge since that musket ball flew yesterday." Nanny clutched the gloves in her lap.

"I heard it hit Calvert's warehouse," Lucy added. Her blue eyes grew large as she looked around the table.

"It fell short and landed in the water," Delany replied. "But that is not the point—"

Sarah, her voice calm, interrupted. "The good news is that no one was injured."

"Yes," Delany continued, "but I've got to do something. I can't just sit here and let them take everything." The militia at Kemp's Landing was the only option. She would go to Kemp's Landing. Lord knew what she could do to help.

"Mr. Spitler says we are to remove to North Carolina immediately upon my return this afternoon. Our effects are already loaded onto the wagons." Lucy stood up and prepared to leave.

Nanny reached out and took Lucy's hands in her own. "Mr. Settle says we will leave also. That shot yesterday was enough for him. He says his wigs will be as welcome in North Carolina as they are here."

"Perhaps we will know each other there?" Lucy trembled. Tears were close behind.

Sarah reached out, and they all joined hands for the last time. "All will be well. We can pray from wherever we are, and we will write to each other."

If the mail gets through. Delany left it unsaid, but they all knew the realities of the current occupation of Norfolk by its royal governor.

"Yes," they chorused together as they tearfully agreed. The ladies walked to the front of the shop, and Nanny and Lucy left together.

Delany still held the door latch when Sarah turned to face her.

"That just leaves us."

"Same time tomorrow?"

Sarah smiled. "Yes."

Delany swung back into her shop looking for something to punch and rushed right into Field Archer's chest. At once surrounded by strong arms and a strong need to bathe, Delany forgot to breathe.

"Aunt Delany," Ben laughed, "Mr. Archer is here

to see you."

"So I see, Ben." She looked up into his twinkling brown eyes and stepped back a proper distance. Of course his height had not changed, but he had filled out. His chest was broad and solid. She pulled her hands back to her chest before she let them slide over to his shoulders. It was Field Archer. He was right here in her shop.

"Mrs. Fleet." His baritone strummed a girlish cord of humiliation that she thought long gone.

Before she could respond, the door opened again.

"Well, Mrs. Fleet, that'll show them, won't it?" John Crawley's fat face was slick with glee. His small black eyes gave her the usual once over that made her feel exposed. She squelched a shudder and moved behind the counter.

Field turned his back to them and moved toward the toy shelves.

"The association will back down now." Crawley wiped his hands down the front of his brown frock coat. "It won't be long before we can get our ships out of here. We are saved, Mrs. Fleet."

"What does his lordship want with a printing press?"

"To silence the dirty-shirts." He hooked his thumbs in the pockets of his coat. "No voice. No followers."

"It remains to be seen, Mr. Crawley, what the militia will do."

"We just saw what those yellow-bellies will do." He bent forward over the counter, enough that she could smell his luncheon ale. "It will all be over soon, and we can get back to business."

"Was there something you needed, Mr. Crawley?" Delany stepped back from the counter and took a glance at Field hoping for an interruption. Seeing only his back, she gazed at the shelf beneath. A new box of wax inserts for missing teeth caught her eye. "Some plumpers for Mrs. Crawley, perhaps?"

The red in Crawley's face deepened to crimson. "No, thank you." He checked his tone. "My mother is in need of nothing at the moment." This time when he leaned in, the gleam in his eye hinted of impropriety.

Delany leaned back.

"Were you frightened?" He rocked back on his heels, looked over his shoulder at Field, rested his elbows on the counter, and breathed a rotten cloud. "I will protect you."

Over my dead body. "Thank you, Mr. Crawley, for your offer, but I can take care of myself." She came out from behind the counter. "Now if there is nothing else, I really shouldn't keep my customers waiting."

After a last glance at her, and then Field, he exited.

Delany wiped the counter of his greasy imprint.

~*~

When the doorbells tinkled, indicating the departure of Mr. Crawley, Field turned toward Mrs. Fleet. The insinuation in Mr. Crawley's declaration of protection gave Field pause. Perhaps his mother had been wrong to send him here.

To be fair, he had kept his back to them to give the man some privacy in his transaction. Any man looking to buy plumpers for his mother would be glad of some privacy. And the glass in which he'd watched their reflections didn't tell a reliable tale. If he read her correctly, she was as repulsed by Crawley as he was infatuated with her. Field thought he saw her look to him for help, but reflections in wavy glass could be distorted. The look in her eye might have been a warning to Crawley to be more guarded in his speech. He needed to watch the next interaction between them to determine their relationship. He couldn't risk his cargo on reminiscences of his mother.

"Mr. Archer, what a surprise to see you here," she said as she tidied her auburn hair with one hand. "Today of all days."

"I just arrived from London."

"Bet you didn't think you would be stepping into this mess."

"Well, I was surprised at the storm damage." He smiled. He had no intention of bringing up the printer and all it meant after the display he'd just seen. "Your place here seems to have been spared." He nodded toward the eighteen-light windows on either side of the door.

Delany Fleet hadn't changed much since he had seen her four years ago at Archer Hall. Certainly, her lavender silk damask gown was of finer material than previously worn on visits to his family home. She wore her own hair piled up on top of her head in the latest fashion with sprigs of curls left out to softly frame her face. Fleet's must be doing well. Certainly, she was doing well for a former servant.

"Yes. I thank God for it." Her voice came out as a sighed release of energy. She raised her silvery eyes to look directly into his. "Is there something I can get for you, Mr. Archer?"

"My mother sent you this." He reached into his pocket and handed her a small parcel wrapped in cloth.

2

Delany accepted the parcel and carefully placed it on the countertop. Wonder displaced the anger and frustration she'd struggled with all day. She untied the ribbon and peeled back the cloth. Inside lay a tiny dress of pink silk and lace.

"My mother was very specific in the shade and style of cut."

"So kind." Mist clouded her eyes. "And so like Mrs. Archer. It's perfect."

"Is one of my mother's creations lying around improperly attired?" He smiled at her again and lounged against the counter.

She smiled back. Field was taller than the odious Crawley, and his effect on her was startling. Instead of threatened, she felt warmed and comforted as if a long-lost friend had come to rescue her from trouble. It had been a strange day. The last person in the colony she would ever consider a friend was Field Archer.

"This is not for one of your mother's dolls. It's for something completely different." The pink silk was so delicate she feared to stain it with her work-dirty fingers. Later, when she was alone, she would take out the doll her mother had made when Delany was four years old and try it on, but she knew it would fit. When God sent a present, it was always exactly right. "Thank you for bringing it to me." She looked up again and found the old playfulness in his warm brown eyes. He hadn't forgotten her after all. At least five years her senior, he had been present on every trip the Fleets had taken to Archer Hall to bring Mrs. Archer the latest in toy innovation.

Delany spent the summer of her fifteenth year dreaming of him. At twenty-seven, she was long over Field Archer and had no desire to go back. It was time she followed her own dreams. She re-wrapped the parcel and placed it in the work basket she always carried home from the shop.

"You are most welcome. Perhaps it will help pave the way for the next question I have to ask you." He stepped back from the counter and looked at the floor. "I have just been to the King's Arms, and because of storm damage, Mrs. Pearse doesn't have room for me to stay. May I stay here until I leave for home? It should only be a couple of days."

No.

He is Ann Archer's oldest son. No one since her father had been as kind to her as Ann Archer. Kemp's Landing would just have to wait.

The back door slapped shut, and Ben came through to the store. Following him was a man Delany had not seen before.

"This is my man, Robert," Field said before she could ask.

"Yes, I can provide a room for you." Delany said.

"But not here. You will have to come to my house where there is a proper bed and a proper bath, and you can be properly fed."

"I don't wish to burden you, Mrs. Fleet."

"Mr. Archer, your mother is dear to me. It is no imposition to give her son a bed for a couple of nights. For propriety's sake, I will make arrangements with my friend, Mrs. Harrison, to stay with us as well. There is room for Robert in the kitchen with the Tabbs." She motioned to Ben. "Go ask Miss Sarah to come for dinner, and tell Mary we will have two guests this evening. And ask Ruben to come to help with Mr. Archer's trunks."

Ben nodded and left by the front door with Robert close behind.

"I shall only require one trunk. I have instructed Robert to place my other cargo in your warehouse if that is convenient."

She readily agreed. Her house was a generous size, but there was hardly storage for four years' worth of trinkets and gifts he must be bringing home to his family.

"I have one more request," Field continued. "Passage home."

"That will be difficult. His majesty's ships control the waterways. It's hard to get through." She rolled her eyes. "They suspect everyone of smuggling arms and ammunition. When they're not busy stealing supplies from the local farms, that is."

"That leaves traveling by coach."

"The committee has the roads tied up. You will

have to get a pass."

"Can you point me in the right direction?"

"I can point. I can't guarantee anything, but I can point."

~*~

The light of dusk set Delany's lavender gown to glow while a stiff breeze relieved the humidity of the day. Field picked up Delany's work basket and offered her his other arm. She took it, but her arm remained rigid against his, creating a six-inch gap.

"I won't attack you, Mrs. Fleet."

A sharp turn of her head, and he was accosted by her remarkable eyes.

"Mr. Archer, if I thought you would attack me, I would hardly offer to entertain you in my home."

He chuckled and walked in the direction she indicated.

"No doubt you are aware of the rules of propriety" Delany said, scanning the street, for what, he didn't know. "I am a widow and toy store owner. I can't afford to have my reputation sullied."

Field glanced at the wooden buildings lining the streets. Most of the shops were closed or closing. Dark interiors silvered the backs of window glass begetting mirrors of the street. Distant singing from a pub in the next street carried on the salty harbor air.

"As quiet as these streets are, I can't imagine anyone seeing anything amiss."

"You have been too long from home, Mr. Archer.

Even the streets have eyes."

Yes, too long, and he wasn't home yet. Norfolk was just a way point. A couple of miles inland, away from the warehouses and muddy streets, where his feet slipped on sandy soil and pine trees loomed overhead, it would feel like home. He wouldn't rest until he had made it to Northumberland County and Archer Hall.

Two blocks from the shop, they left the dusty, dried-mud road and stepped onto the only paved thoroughfare in Norfolk. A short distance led to a cobbled sidewalk and up to a large brick house.

The setting afternoon sun warmed the spacious front hall through windows surrounding the door. A staircase led to the top of the house. Immediately to the left lay a large parlor dominated by two tall bookcases full of volumes.

"You're a reader."

"Does that surprise you?"

A tall, pregnant woman arrived from the back of the house. She wore the brown calico dress of a servant.

"Miss Delany." The woman nodded and took Delany's bag. "Miss Sarah said she'd be along for supper. I have water prepared for the waterfall. It won't have had enough time to warm."

"Thank you, Mary." Delany turned to him. "Follow Mary. She'll show you to the mechanical waterfall."

"You have a waterfall?"

"Yes. Mary will show you. It might be a little cold,

but I find it refreshing on days like these."

Field followed Mary through the hallway out to the back porch where Robert waited. On the porch stood a tall wooden closet. At the top of the closet rested a small cistern. He had heard of these contraptions, of course, but he had yet to use one. How interesting to find someone in a provincial colony with such a device. On the other hand, where else would it be more practical than in hot and humid Norfolk?

"You stand in there, pull this chain to get yourself wet," Robert said, "and then wash. Once you are done washing, pull the chain and rinse yourself." Robert handed him a towel and a cake of soap. His banyan and slippers rested on a small bench next to the closet.

Field stepped into the closet to remove his clothes.

Delany Fleet intrigued him. Like her shop, she was full of odd curiosities. Much more than the young girls continually introduced to him in London. Field wanted a wife, and if he could have found someone to love with an ounce of sense among the lilies in bloom in London, he would have married her. Meeting Delany again confirmed what he'd been thinking as he'd left England to come home. His wife should be home grown. Unfortunately, the only woman in Virginia ever interested in him was Simon's sister, Hester. He winced at the thought. *Horsey Hester*. He wasn't that desperate. No. Love was what he wanted. Love for each other made his parents' marriage different from most of the others he'd seen. He could hold out until he found the right woman.

He set his clothes on the bench outside and pulled

the chain. By the time he stepped out, his teeth were chattering, and his fingertips were blue. Clean? Yes. Refreshing? No. In his room, he found Robert had laid out his midnight blue frock coat and buff breeches for dinner.

Downstairs, he rejoined his hostess in the parlor. She, too, was dressed for dinner in a soft grey gown that accented her eyes and clear complexion and contrasted the rose of her lips. The curly spins of auburn hair had been tamed and returned to her simple knot. He deliberately turned his gaze to the other woman in the room.

"Mr. Archer, may I present my dear friend, Mrs. Harrison."

Mrs. Harrison, trim and prim in black broadcloth, looked good for a woman of late forties or early fifties. He'd wager her clear blue eyes didn't miss much. He bowed. "Mrs. Harrison."

Ben, clean and dressed in a brown suit, stood by a window.

Field nodded to the boy and received a nod in return.

Once Mary gestured to Delany, the company moved across the hall to the dining room.

Delany sat at the head of the long oval table; to her left, Mrs. Harrison. Field was offered the seat to her right, and Ben sat next to him.

When Mary, with Ruben to assist, had set down platters of ham and chicken, a plate of cornbread, bowls of fruit and greens, they stood by seats at the foot of the table.

Field stifled his surprise.

"Where is Robert?" Delany asked.

"He didn't feel comfortable sitting here with us, so with your permission, we will join him in the kitchen," Ruben answered.

"Very well. It won't do to make him uncomfortable."

"Do your servants usually eat with you?" Field asked. Intellectually, he could concede, as Mr. Wesley asserted, that all people were entitled to access to God. All humans could and should receive Christ. But surely that did not mean one had to eat with one's servants. Did his mother know of this?

"Only dinner. The rest of the time, we are all just too busy."

"Mr. Archer," Sarah injected, "Mrs. Fleet tells me that your mother carves the dolls that Mrs. Fleet sells in her shop."

"Yes, ma'am, she does."

"I have given one of your mother's dolls to each of my four granddaughters. They are prized possessions, I can tell you."

"My mother will be glad to hear it." Indeed, her letters had been full of elation for her new vocation. "But I've been wondering for some time how Mrs. Fleet convinced my very private mother to display her works in a shop. In Norfolk, no less. Is not Williamsburg considered more refined?"

"Perhaps, Mr. Archer, your mother preferred to take a risk where she was less known," Delany responded.

"I find it curious that my mother should display her work at all."

"That you will have to take up with Mrs. Archer," Delany said. "But I will say this: toys are far more useful items than people give them credit for. I believe a curious mind is a healthy mind, and the more one uses it to solve puzzles of one kind or another the better."

"You have made a study of the subject?" Field paused for her answer.

"Not in the way you suggest, but I have long observed the effects of toys on my customers."

"Perhaps you should commission a study to be undertaken or perhaps undertake the study yourself."

"Perhaps I should indeed." She teased him with a grin.

"Mrs. Fleet, how did you come by a mechanical waterfall?"

"I read about it, and I thought it would be a godsend in the Virginia heat."

"It certainly does cool off a person."

"You weren't too cold, were you?" Concern softened her eyes from silver to gray. "I've come out of there with my teeth chattering." Her face lit with merriment. "Mary will usually put fresh water in there in the morning so it has time to warm up a little before I use it. She didn't have time today."

"I heard John Holt was hiding in his office the whole time the soldiers were in there, and they didn't find him." Ben's outburst of enthusiasm reminded him of himself at thirteen. He begged his father to let him go fight with Washington in the French and Indian War.

"Folks are saying that Lord Dunmore will free the slaves and the indentured," Mrs. Harrison said. "One would think his lordship was looking for war."

"He should free the slaves," Delany said. "Indenture is an entirely different thing, of course."

His mind scrambled. "Do you side with the King?" He would have to find someone else to help him. The trunks should be safe in her warehouse until tomorrow. Then he would have to make other arrangements.

"I didn't say that I side with Lord Dunmore or his king. I said that slavery should be outlawed."

"But you think it is acceptable for his lordship to take the property of freeborn men?"

"No. I think the plundering that he has done on local plantations is outrageous. However, people were created by God and should never be property. Therefore, in my estimation, it is perfectly sound that he should free people who should never be enslaved in the first place."

"Do you think he intends that they will remain free?"

The flash in her eyes told him she hadn't thought of that. "I don't know."

"But you do know that indentures are different?"

The confusion cleared on her face, "Oh, yes. People indenture themselves of their own free will. It's a contract that they make with their employer."

"So you don't find that hard?"

"Some masters are hard. Yes. But how is the system itself any different from a man hiring out as a clerk in someone's office and being paid a daily wage?" Delany tore a piece of cornbread and lathered it with butter. "Our own indenture proved quite profitable for my father and me."

He could hardly argue with a former indentured servant about indentured servitude.

"Where do you stand on independence, Mrs. Fleet?"

"Independence of whom, Mr. Archer?" She took a sip of water and skewered him with a glinty, silver look. "If you speak of women, I'm all for it. I believe women should be allowed to participate in the process by which they are governed. And to sell the efforts of their creativity should they so choose."

"Especially when they contribute financially to the benefit of the communities in which they live," Mrs. Hamilton added.

"Precisely," Delany said. "Where do you stand on the independence of women, Mr. Archer?" The impish look in her countenance confused him. Was she teasing him, or had she deftly but deliberately evaded his question?

3

Sitting at her desk in the cool early morning with her Bible in the quiet, establishing her connection with her Lord, was the source of Delany's strength. This morning she could feel Field Archer upstairs pulling her thoughts from what she needed to accomplish. She closed the Bible.

What is it about that man that makes my house feel crowded?

Perhaps if she concentrated on work, she could focus her thoughts. Mr. Harris had brought the papers necessary to release the Tabbs from their indenture, and she needed to review them to confirm that all was in order.

Delany had heard the rumors of Lord Dunmore's threat long before Sarah had brought it up at dinner last night. It was time to free Mary and Ruben from their agreement. Initially planned to be a gift when the baby came, there was no time for that now. The land agreed upon was the same land Delany and her father had earned from the elder Mr. Fleet, her father-in-law. It adjoined the property that Ben's father, Samuel, still farmed. Her heart warmed at the thought of Ruben and Mary in their very own home when their baby came. She tucked the papers away in her basket. Tomorrow she would stop by Mr. Harris's to sign them in front of witnesses.

"Chocolate, Miss Delany?" Mary slipped in with a tray. "Will you be attending services this morning?"

"Yes." Delany took the cup of chocolate from the tray to let it warm her cupped hands. "If Mr. Archer is not up when we leave, you may leave breakfast on the sideboard for him."

Mary nodded and left the room.

Delany reached for a piece of toast and gazed out the window into the garden beyond. A mist clung to the shady ground near the fence line. It would be another hot day.

The ache for a child of her own was no longer a surprise. As Mary's child grew larger, Delany's longing grew deeper. She had never loved Tom and didn't believe she could love any man so much that she was willing to give away her freedom again.

But a child was a different story. It was too late now, but she knew she would have loved her own child as she loved Ben. He excelled at his apprenticeship and would be a worthy heir. Now she had to get him home to Princess Anne County where he would be safe with his father and mother. She would go to Kemp's Landing and do what she could to help the militia.

Delany's library was positioned in such a way that she could view the stairs and hall without being observed, at least to those unfamiliar with its layout. Field, in a forest green frock coat and buff breeches, came down the stairs for breakfast, and Delany couldn't help but stare at the fluid and graceful way he moved. He walked into the dining room and immediately came back out again headed toward her library. He scanned the book-lined walls before addressing her. "Impressive."

"Is it the library or the fact that it belongs to a woman that impresses you, Mr. Archer?" She couldn't seem to stop heckling him and didn't know why. He was leaving in a couple of days, and then her life could go back to normal.

Raised eyebrows and twinkling brown eyes, he answered, "I'll admit to both." He smiled broadly. "The women of my most recent acquaintance disliked the smell of libraries."

"Then they need new cleaning staff."

He laughed out loud at her comment, and she smiled at him.

"May I escort you to services this morning?" Field asked.

Delany hesitated. She was going to the service, and they could go together. Did that mean he had to escort her? She supposed it did. "Yes, you may." She stood. "You will find breakfast in the dining room. I will join you shortly." She looked up.

He smiled at her and left the room. He might think her flighty, but she needed some space from him. She had things of her own to do, and they didn't include a stranger from the past who couldn't see past her indenture.

~*~

Sarah was always a late riser. Delany was just about to send Mary to see if Sarah would accompany them to church when Sarah flew down the stairs, slippers clattering on the polished wood. Sarah stopped short when she saw everyone assembled by the door.

Delany smiled. "We were just leaving."

"I'm ready." Sarah, breathing in gasps, walked stately the rest of the way down.

Ben offered his arm to Sarah.

Mary and Ruben followed them out the door.

Field offered his arm to Delany.

Once again, Delany kept a rigid distance from Field. The way to the Borough Church took them back through Market Square and up Church Street. Rolled lumps of dried mud fought her feet. Lord Dunmore had called it a "dirty borough," and she could see his point. She walked more in her pattens than out of them. What the borough lacked in beauty, it made up for in energy. It bustled with people who were building things, selling things, buying things. Norfolk had it all. Today, it rested—except for the steady throng leaving the threat of his Lordship's gun boats.

~*~

Church Street, the only road out of town, also housed the church. Wagons full of household goods lumbered by them. Mothers and fathers watching and corralling crying babies and playing children made their way down the street.

Field placed his hand over Delany's on his arm and stepped quickly in front of Ben and Mrs. Harrison as much to protect them as to provide a way through the confusion of people.

Mr. Crawley, in a suit of black broadcloth, stood near the door of the church with an older woman Field assumed was his mother. The older woman was dressed like her son in somber broadcloth with the addition of frothy white lace.

Delany tensed under his touch when she caught sight of the pair. He once again placed his hand over hers.

She relaxed the distance between them.

"Mrs. Fleet, I see you are not alone," Mr. Crawley said looking at Field, who stood at least a head taller than the merchant.

"Mr. Crawley, Mrs. Crawley, I would like you to meet an old family friend, Mr. Field Archer."

Field nodded a bow and smiled at them.

"An old family friend." Crawley's dark eyes took in every inch of Delany's indigo gown.

Delany stepped closer to Field and stiffened.

"I wonder you didn't introduce us yesterday." Mr. Crawley sneered.

"Come along, John. We'll be late." The command issued by his mother brought him to her side.

Field navigated them to Delany's pew box directly in front of the Crawley's, and he moved through the motions of the service thinking only of Delany's reaction to Crawley. *What hold did he have over her?*

He leaned over and whispered, "We need to talk."

Reverend Black introduced his guest as a minister from Pennsylvania. The guest spoke of the unrest around them as a coming revolution. That was dangerous talk in a town that seemed so loyal to the king.

Field had stood in the crowd as they'd done nothing when the printer's press had been confiscated. The men present could easily have overpowered the few soldiers Lord Dunmore had sent. Had this minister been there as well?

"We have heard that the crown has a black list of some of our most trusted representatives in the Assembly in Williamsburg. There is reason to believe that at the first sign of trouble, those leaders will be sought out and apprehended. Shall we do nothing?" the minister asked.

Field's heart froze at the words resounding from the pulpit. If they were true, his father was in danger. And if Lord Dunmore knew that Reed Archer's son was under his nose, Field wouldn't stand a chance. He had to act quickly. At the last syllable of the final blessing, Field motioned toward the entrance of the box.

Delany took his cue and led the way out.

In the aisle, he was introduced to Sarah Harrison's children and grandchildren as well as the Parkers and the Harris family and others he would never remember.

They smiled at him and complimented his mother. He nodded and smiled back. After thirty minutes of meeting and greeting, they finally reached the door and stepped outside.

"Mrs. Fleet, would you walk with me over the bridge?"

She took his arm and with the rigid distance back in place between them, they headed the long way home. The day was warm, but a breeze blew off the water that kept it tolerable.

"About Mr. Crawley," he started.

She pulled her arm from his and interlaced her fingers. "I owe you an apology for the way I exaggerated our connection to the Crawleys."

"It is of no consequence. My mother speaks quite warmly of you. That alone certainly elevates you closer to our family than any other merchant I know." Her gaze flew to his; a guarded relief warmed their silver depths.

"Mr. Crawley suffers from the delusion that I will marry him."

The thought of her in Crawley's greasy arms repulsed him. He took a deep breath. She was entitled to do what she wished with her life. "Shall you?"

"Absolutely not." She shuddered.

"Then what hold does he have over you?"

"He was a friend of my late husband. When Tom died within a few days of his father, Mr. Crawley helped me get on my feet. Not financially, you understand. That was all taken care of. But he helped me keep the store open, so he thinks he's entitled to me." She wrapped her arms around herself and shivered. "He is personally acquainted with Lord

Dunmore and is willing to denounce anyone he thinks supports the militia."

"Then Reverend Black's guest had better run."

"He doesn't care about a mere minister. It's money he's after. He wants my store and anything else he can get for cheap."

The lust for money was not what Field had seen in Crawley's eye when he looked at Delany Fleet.

The bridge over Back Creek was wide enough for one wagon and a pedestrian path on one side.

Field offered his arm once more.

Delany took it.

"I need to leave soon if our guest speaker was correct."

"Your father."

"Before I say anymore, I need the truth from you."

She halted.

"I always tell the truth." She looked down. "Mostly always." She smiled back at him, an impish look in the silver.

"Where do you stand on independency?"

"Until two days ago, I found it a nuisance. Men scrabbling over something that I can't control. Then someone from the *King Fisher* fired a musket into the borough."

"Was anyone hurt?"

She shook her head. "We were told it was an accident. I don't believe in accidents. It's time for me to take Ben home."

"Where is that?"

"Princess Anne County."

"You still haven't answered my question."

They had arrived on Talbot Street and were close to her home.

"The streets have eyes and ears, Mr. Archer. Would you care for luncheon?"

Once inside, she escorted him to her library.

"I am going to join the militia."

He laughed out loud at her suggestion. Schoolboys were bigger than the petite woman who barely reached his collar.

"Don't you dare laugh," she said pointing a finger at him. "I am a practical woman, Field Archer." She turned to pace. "I can't shoot like a foot soldier, but I'm a merchant with a reputation. It may not work for long…"

"Perhaps we can help each other."

She stopped pacing. "How?"

"I have something that I need to deliver to Williamsburg."

"I'm going in the opposite direction."

"What I have will help the militia, and the militia can help me get what I have to the right place."

"You told me you wanted the truth from me," she said.

He nodded.

"Tell me the truth. What is it we are talking about?"

He hesitated. If he told her the truth, she might refuse to help. If he didn't, she would refuse to help. In either case, he felt sure she wouldn't turn him in if only for his mother's sake.

"I have four cases of flintlocks."

She stiffened, and her eyes glinted.

"Do you mean to tell me that you have smuggled weapons into my warehouse?" Her voice was dangerously low. "That you put my family in danger without so much as a—a—" She balled her fists and raised them to his chest.

He stepped back.

She swung by him and went to the window. She placed one hand on a pane of glass as she struggled for composure.

Cool guilt snaked his abdomen and squeezed. She was right; he'd had no plan. He had given no thought to his father's request for weapons. He'd bought them through his London contacts and brought them home.

"Are you always reckless?" Her voice remained low as she turned toward him.

"Reckless is not the word I would choose."

"What you have done could've had monumental consequences for my family if your guns were discovered in my warehouse. Big consequences require well-thought-out plans." Hands balled into fists shook with restraint at her sides. Silver sparked with fire pierced him.

"'The wind blows where it listeth…'" he quoted from John's Gospel. He relaxed his body and raised his hands. "Trust me."

She gasped.

"Trust. You?" Surprised outrage creased her features. A ridiculous laugh escaped her lips and released the tension in her body. Delany took a deep breath. "I'd sooner trust a walking rattlesnake."

4

Delany's father, James Button, had been the last person to make her angry enough to laugh. It only happened when she was livid, and the tension threatened to break into violence. Then, from somewhere deep within her spirit, laughter would bubble up. Instantaneously, her perspective would change. So it was now.

They both turned at the soft tap on the door.

"Luncheon is served," Mary said.

Field motioned her forward.

Delany led the way to the dining room.

Sarah and Ben had already arrived.

Once seated, Delany asked Ben to bless the food. Still too tense to eat, Delany took a small portion of chicken pie. Archer's portion was twice her own. Apparently, arguments didn't curb his appetite, but he wasn't unfazed. She watched as he deliberately relaxed his anger-hardened contours before he engaged Ben.

"Mrs. Tabb is a superior cook," he said. "This chicken pie is the best I've tasted since I've been gone."

"You should taste her maids-of-honor," Ben said between mouthfuls. "She always makes them after she makes the apple jelly."

"They melt in your mouth," Sarah added.

Delany inclined her head in agreement, thankful that calm, dependable Sarah was there to carry the conversation.

She had told Field of her plan to join the militia not two minutes before he informed her of his flintlocks. It wasn't the opportunity to help that made her angry. Rather, it was the brazen assumption he could bring smuggled goods to her house. The forcing of her hand. The lack of choice. That made her angry. It was just like Tom, who thought he could do as he wished with her property just because he was her husband. As though she and her father had not worked the seven years to earn the land. Seven years' work—gone with a name scribbled on a piece of paper that said, "Certificate of Marriage."

Never again.

'The wind,' indeed. Could he not see the fact of the guns in her warehouse made her guilty of smuggling? Lord Dunmore wouldn't care where they came from—only that they were in her warehouse. And Ben? Was she supposed to move guns with Ben?

"Is that all right with you, Aunt?"

Ben's question brought her back to the table.

"Is what all right?"

"After dinner, I'll show Mr. Archer around town."

"Stay away from the waterfront. You don't know when that fool will start taking pot shots at us." It would be more than all right to get Field Archer out of her house for a while so she could think how to proceed. "And mind the clouds. It looks like rain."

"Keep your eyes about you," Sarah said. "The streets aren't as safe as they used to be with the soldiers running around as if they own the place."

"I'll keep an eye on him," Archer said.

Delany had just retreated to her library after man and boy departed when Sarah entered.

"I must speak with you."

They sat together on the cream sofa by the window that overlooked her garden.

"Do you care for coffee or chocolate?"

"Neither." Sarah slouched back on the couch, hands fisted at her side. "I want a cup of tea!"

"Don't we all." Delany rang for Mary.

The embargo on tea had been in effect for over a year. There was none to be had in the shops or anywhere else. Except for the one small box Delany had hidden.

"Mary, please bring a pot of tea for Mrs. Harrison."

Mary's eyes bulged.

Sarah exhaled loudly. "I'll have coffee. I don't think I could take another drop of 'liber-tea.'"

Delany reached out and gave a reassuring pat to Sarah's hand.

Lightning lit clouds outside the window, and thunder cracked.

"My son tells me that he is taking his family away from here to his brother's farm in Pungo." The usual calm voice trembled in distress. "He insists that I come with them. He says he will not allow me stay here alone."

Mary returned and placed a tea tray laden with a coffeepot, two cups, and an assortment of tea cakes on a nearby table.

Delany poured a steaming cup for Sarah and one for herself.

Sarah inhaled the fragrant brew. "Delany Fleet. Where did you get this tea?" She clutched her bosom, her voice a hoarse whisper. "You're not dealing with smugglers?"

"Of course not. I find I like my morning chocolate at least as much as I like tea, so I saved it. Don't get too excited. I don't have much."

Sarah closed her eyes inhaling the smell. Black market, indeed. Delany couldn't deny a definite pull to trade in much wanted goods no matter where they came from, but that was more danger than she was willing to risk. Oddly enough, it was true. She had grown used to her morning chocolate and hadn't missed her beloved tea of late. Still, it was a blessing to sit here with her only friend and drink tea as they had so many times in the past.

"I told George that I was staying with you for as long as Mr. Archer is here." She took another sip. "I knew he would like the idea that there was a big, strong man around."

Delany didn't want to think about Field Archer being big and strong. The way he filled up a room was positively stifling.

"We have Ruben. We don't need to depend on Mr. Archer."

Sarah focused her calm blue eyes on Delany. "Yes,

but Ruben belongs to Mary."

Delany sipped tea and selected a tea cake.

Sarah's usual cool voice returned. "It might be time for you to think about marrying again."

Delany chomped into the cake, causing it to crumble down her dress. "How can you say that when you just bristled at what George will allow?"

"I don't wish to leave my house. I love my son and daughter-in-law, but I like the freedom of living alone. But that's not the same thing. You're still a young woman. It's not too late for you to have a family of your own."

"In order to have a family of my own, I would have to marry."

"Tom was not the man for you, Delany. But that doesn't mean that God can't send you a man who is the perfect match for you."

A picture of Field as he was when she was fifteen filled her memory. A teasing sparkle in his brown eyes. The wide smile that welcomed her presence.

She's just a servant.

"Those days are gone, Sarah. I'm a rich widow, and I don't need a husband."

"My son Isaac is still alone with his little Lucy. You love Lucy."

"Of course I love Lucy. But you know that Isaac and I are just friends."

"She just turned four." Sarah's smile warmed her face.

"It's not like you to be so forward." Delany reached for the older woman's hand. "Isaac won't appreciate your matchmaking, let alone pairing him with me. I'm not what he needs."

"Oh, what does he know about it? I'm worried about him. It's been three years since Polly died."

"He'll find his way." Delany returned Sarah's hand with a reassuring squeeze.

"I know you're right. But what about you? What about children?"

"What? People who will allow me to stay in my own home?" She laughed. "No, thank you. I have Ben."

"If you stay here, I won't be alone."

Dismay wafted through Delany's heart. She hadn't given much thought to what it would mean to her friend if she left and joined the militia. If she could just have a few minutes alone, she could begin to plan and account for those very types of details.

Returning Ben to Princess Anne took precedence over all else. Delany didn't know what assistance she could offer the ragamuffin band of Minutemen. She just needed to do something.

Field Archer's problem offered the opportunity to do something more quickly than she'd had time to think. Ideas shot around her brain faster than she could capture them. First, she would have to inform Archer of her decision to help him. Then she would start on her list.

Thunder rattled the window panes. Clouds let go the rain. A cold breeze blew through the cracks in the casements. The front door banged open. A quick glance confirmed the return of Archer and Ben. Boots scuffled up the stairs.

"Sarah, I have to bring Ben home. Will you travel with me? After we drop him at his home, we could travel on to Pungo."

A resigned look on her face, Sarah said, "Of course I will."

~*~

"It must've dropped ten degrees in the last hour," Field announced upon entering the drawing room, which had not grown dark enough for candles but murky enough to strain the eyes. He took a seat by the empty fireplace. Blank faces of the two ladies stared back at him. Mrs. Harrison went back to her knitting. Mrs. Fleet, ensconced at a cherry wood secretary with a stack of foolscap, dipped her quill in the ink pot and scratched across the page. He turned his gaze toward the windows and the storm coming down.

Frustration chewed at his composure. The boxes must be removed from Mrs. Fleet's warehouse, and they must be delivered to Williamsburg. The sooner the better, and before Lord Dunmore or one of his minions discovered he was the son of a member of the shadow government now running Virginia. He had no desire to return to England aboard one of His Lordship's sloops-of-war.

The difficulties surrounding this otherwise simple task confounded him. His father would never have sent him knowingly into danger; therefore, the situation was worse than when Reed Archer had sent the request. He'd confirmed Mrs. Fleet's assessment when he and Ben had surveyed the harbor. It was infested with British sloops and tenders. Travel by boat was not possible without detection. Overland was the only option.

The estimable Mrs. Pearse, owner of The King's Arms, didn't have any horses left to hire. So many people had left the borough that she retained only those horses she stabled.

It seemed all he could do was wait. He stood and walked the length of the room.

The only light in this gloom had been Delany's nephew Ben. He'd turned out to be an informative guide. His devotion to his aunt was commendable.

His aunt, on the other hand, was a conundrum. One minute she was an ardent patriot telling him how she was joining the militia and fight for freedom. The next minute, she was a wintery adversary blaming him for putting her family in danger. Did she not see helping him helped the militia? It was just plain unreasonable. But then again, he'd never found women to be reasonable creatures. He placed his hands on either side of the window.

Water flowed in rivulets down the cobbles of the street.

There was one good outcome from this unexpected detour: his search for a wife was taking on clarity. The ideal bride had been a bit vague before his re-acquaintance with Delany Fleet. A girl from home would be reasonable and follow his guidance—something the socialites he'd met in London would never do. He would be the master of his home, and his bride would help him. They would enjoy quiet evenings by a fireside discussing the latest farming techniques and the fascinating results of his experiments. Children puddled around their feet at night would walk beside him during the day learning as he had done from his father about Archer Hall.

The clouds hung dark and distended with rain. They would have to light the candles soon. At this point, the day would not lighten again.

"Mr. Archer, I would speak with you." Mrs. Fleet's voice cracked the silence in the room. He turned to see her gathering the sheets of foolscap. "If you have a moment."

No lightness in the serious gray eyes.

"I am at your service, Mrs. Fleet."

She sat behind her desk in the library and motioned him to a chair placed before her. He sat down and crossed his legs and arms and placed one finger on his lips.

"I'm not a schoolboy, Mrs. Fleet."

Her cheeks bloomed a cheery shade of rose. "And I am no longer a servant, Mr. Archer." She straightened the foolscap. "This is my desk, and you are my guest. And we have business to discuss." She fixed her gaze on him. "I've decided to help you."

He raised an eyebrow.

"Just how are you planning to do that?"

"First, we travel together to Princess Anne to deliver Ben to his parents." He caught her gaze. "We can leave your cargo at Fleets for a day while we deliver Sarah—Mrs. Harrison—to her son in Pungo." A slight inclination of his head and she continued. "After that, we return to Fleet farm, and you go on to Archer Hall. I will come home."

"Pearse has no horses."

"Pearse had better still have my horses."

Relief surged through him like a stimulating brew. That was the answer. He'd wrongly assumed she'd hire horses when she needed them. Too bad he hadn't thought to ask Ben. He stood. "It's best if I go alone. I'll tell Robert to prepare to leave in the morning." He headed toward the door.

"No."

"Surely, you can see the folly of so many people traveling with my boxes. Especially Ben."

"Surely, you can see the necessity of removing my nephew from Norfolk posthaste. And I am sure that you have ascertained that my horses are all I have to transport my nephew." Rising behind her desk, she rested her fingertips on its shining surface. "I cannot leave the boxes here and bring Ben home and come back again due to the risk of them being found. I cannot risk his safety by leaving him here in favor of some inanimate objects." She took a deep breath and sat down again. "There you are. I have no choice. I must remove Ben and your boxes at once. Together."

"That's a lot of driving around with my boxes. How sure are you that we'll not get caught?"

"That is your problem. I will provide credentials required by the committee to travel. You provide protection."

"I'll be prepared to leave at first light."

She laughed, and the girl he'd teased resurfaced. He paused for a beat as he remembered why he used to tease her.

"It will take me two days at least to prepare to leave. Can you be ready in two days?"

"Obviously."

"Assuming the rain lets up. We aren't going anywhere until the streets dry out."

5

Dawn came late through the fog into Delany's library window. Mary and Ruben would meet her shortly. With so many people in the house she surmised that meeting them early would ensure their privacy. They arrived with a tray of chocolate and three cups as she had instructed. Delany sat on the settee and offered two wing chairs for her guests.

Ruben waited for Mary to sit before he sat clutching his hat in his hands.

Delany poured chocolate.

"I have some news that will change a great many things for us," she said.

Ruben wrung his hat.

Mary slid closer to the edge of her chair.

"Whatever it is, Miss Delany," Ruben took Mary's hand, "we'll take care of you."

Mary shook her head in agreement.

Delany's heart was full. Oh, how she would miss them. They had worked beside her since Tom died, more companions than servants.

"I believe the time has come to return Ben to his parents." She folded her hands together in her lap. "My plan is to leave here as soon as I can. I would like you both to accompany me."

Their clasped hands tightened as they agreed with each other.

Mary frowned, "Of course we will, Miss Delany. Wherever you go, we will go with you."

"I am so thankful to God for you both." Delany's eyes pricked with tears. She took a deep breath. "I have some papers here that I will give to you later after I have signed them before witnesses, but I wanted you to see them now." She handed them to Ruben for inspection.

Mary read over their clasped hands.

"Miss Delany, we still have a year with you. You don't need to do this," Ruben said.

Delany looked down at the well-polished floor.

"Ruben Tabb, the Lord has made it plain to me that now is the time." She looked directly into the honest man's deep brown eyes. "Just think about what's going on around us. I hear threats to burn Norfolk from one side or the other every day. We can't keep our vulnerable ones here any longer." She cast a glance at Mary; Ruben followed her gaze.

Mary sat up straight. "Oh no. You don't need to worry about me. I can take care of myself."

"Raids have started," Ruben said softly still looking at the papers in his hands. "I heard soldiers say they're searching for gunpowder."

"I planned to do this when the baby came anyway."

"I don't know what to say, Miss Delany." The sun shone in Ruben's face when he looked up again.

Mary still looked concerned. "Who will take care of you, Miss Delany?"

Delany took a deep breath. "I know it's time to take Ben home and bring you home. I want to come back here. But whatever happens, I know that God will take care of me. He always does."

"Do you think they'll confiscate the house?"

Delany grew faint. "I hope not. If it burns, I lose everything. If it's confiscated, I can try to fight it with Mr. Harris." She looked out the window at the gray day. "I don't know what else to do. We cannot know what the future will bring. I cannot keep Ben here. I cannot travel with him alone." She raised her hands.

Ruben nodded. "So be it."

Mary and Ruben left the room still holding hands.

In the hallway where Ruben obviously thought he couldn't be heard, he whispered to his wife, "We're going home."

"Home," echoed Mary.

Home? Delany hadn't thought of home in such a long time. The house she had shared with her father in London was nothing but a floor plan and vague swatches of color now. Since coming to the colony, she and her father had lived with the Fleets, sharing a room until it was no longer seemly. They occupied separate rooms after that. They'd not had a home to call their own. James Button died just after their new home had been built. Then she'd lived with Tom. Home was not a building. Home was with her father.

Armed with her list and work basket containing the release papers for the Tabbs, Delany clattered through the rain in her pattens. A drizzly mist congealed moisture on everything. Even an umbrella couldn't protect her from this kind of rain. She clutched her basket close to her chest to shield the papers from the dampness.

The Tabbs were going home. Tom's brother Samuel and his wife Molly were the only family Delany had left in Virginia. Samuel was a steady man without the cold arrogance of his sibling. Molly had always made her feel welcome. She could trust them. They would listen and help her decide what she needed to do next. Stay in Norfolk or move to Northumberland.

Delany stood to lose her only income if Norfolk burned down. What she'd told Sarah was true. She had wealth, but it wouldn't last forever. Ideally, the farm in Northumberland would start producing before she sold the shop and left Norfolk. Every day, threats of burning the borough made their way to her store. No one was surprised that Lord Dunmore would burn them out, but now their own militia had added their voice to the threat. The rumored motivations were said to be to keep the British from getting a foothold on Norfolk's harbor and to punish the Tories. Outrage was her response. Did any of them think of the people involved with all this destruction they were planning? Fleet's Toys had occupied the same space for the last seventy-five years. All could be gone in a spark. It made her shiver.

The sight of the cheery little shop warmed away her cold, gloomy thoughts. She opened up the door to find Ann's dolls on the top shelves still smiled a greeting. Tiny cups and saucers awaited tea. Noah's animals still mingled freely outside their ark. Newfangled puzzles sat in their boxes waiting to show the way to new places.

It was ten o'clock now. In an hour, she would walk down to see David Harris. Until then, she would pack up the most important parts of her inventory. Some she would take home; others, like Ann's dolls, would go with her to Princess Anne.

She was perched on a ladder reaching for a doll on the top shelf when the front doorbells jingled, and John Crawley entered.

"Mrs. Fleet." His tone dripped wantonness.

Dear God, don't let him touch me. She gripped the ladder tightly and climbed down quickly, before he could trap her.

"Allow me," his voice was closer now.

Anger strengthened her resolve as the reality of what he must be thinking of her derrière swinging in his direction filtered into her mind. Her feet were on the floor before he could ask her again. She took a glance at the small timepiece pinned to the bodice of her dress. "Mr. Crawley, I must apologize. I have an appointment in exactly thirty minutes. What may I do to help you this morning?"

"I have come to discuss a matter of some importance."

A chill gripped Delany's heart, and she clasped her hands together. *Not now.* It had been coming for some time. She'd known that, but not now. She bustled over to stand next to the counter to provide space between them. Guilt embroidered the edges of her resolve. She did not wish to witness his embarrassment.

"Mrs. Fleet," Crawley paused to wipe his hands down the front of his coat, "may I call you Delany?" He closed his eyes and continued without her consent, "Delany, when my excellent friend Tom married you, a woman who had been indentured to his house, I cautioned him." He opened his eyes and began to pace the room. "'Tom,' I said, 'don't do it. You'll be miserable.'" He took a deep breath and paused his pacing, "But it was I who was wrong."

Delany gripped the counter.

"Yes, my dear Delany, it was I who was wrong. I watched your marriage. And after Tom died, we became friends." He continued moving about wiping a finger here and there across her shelves. "It has been some time that I have been desirous of a wife. Now that a decent interval has passed since Tom's death, I think it's time."

Despite the forewarning, Delany's heart sank.

He moved toward her. "I have come to ask for your consent to be my wife, my dearest Delany Fleet." He reached out to grasp her hand.

Delany retracted to the farthest reach of her counter and took a deep breath. She had no wish to hurt him, but that didn't change her feelings or her estimation of his character. The greed and mean-spiritedness she'd seen grow in him not only repulsed her, it frightened. The lecherous look in his eyes got worse every day. He coveted her store. He didn't want her.

"Mr. Crawley, I am sorry." She faltered, "I have no wish to hurt you. You did come to my aid in a time of crisis." She tried to look at him kindly.

He smiled and nodded. Apparently, he hadn't heard the first part of what she said.

"I cannot marry you."

Crimson rose in his fat cheeks, and his dark eyes turned to rock. "It's because of that Mr. Archer, isn't it?" A lustful gleam now glowed in his dark eyes. "I saw how you hung on to him yesterday."

"My friendship with Mr. Archer's family is none of your business."

He backed up from the counter and turned as if to leave then lurched around to face her again. "You don't think that he will marry the likes of you, do you?" He laughed. "Gentry like him don't come looking for wives among the servants." Cold laughter rang again. "You're naught but a servant and always will be. Despite this store and whatever trimmings you put on." He waved his arm in front of her and stepped in close.

She turned her head to deflect the stench of his breath.

"You and I are the same type, Delany Fleet. We work for money." His mouth widened to a broad grin. "He's too good for the likes of you." He grinned at her again before he turned and left.

Delany waved her hands in front of her face to dispel the trailing smell John Crawley left in his wake.

How could so young a man smell so dissipated? He was not much older than she was, about the same age as Field Archer. But what a difference. John had been very kind when Tom died, showing her how the ledgers worked and other necessities of running a store. He had changed in the last couple of years.

Married.

To Field Archer.

Her face warmed as a wisp of the old dream paraded before her eyes. Of course he would never marry a servant. She glanced at her watch. It was eleven. She would be late. She ran around back to find Ruben, with Ben alongside, just five steps from the back door. "I'm late for my appointment with Mr. Harris." Delany picked up her basket and headed out the door. She took a deep breath. At least it was behind her now.

John Crawley wouldn't come knocking on her door again.

~*~

The rain was dreary, but it could prove a useful companion after all. Outside work must wait while clouds wrung themselves of moisture. Perhaps he could gain some much-needed information by simply loitering near those who were usually more gainfully employed.

The King's Arms was doing a hearty business despite the still visible storm damage to the upper floor of the establishment. Archer weaved his way through boisterous sailors sharing a meal, ducked just in time to miss a blow from a man waving a newspaper in a heated discussion, and slipped through a doorway into a smaller room. He took a seat at a table by a window as far as he could get from the clamor.

"You must be Archer." A portly, ruddy-faced gentleman dressed in an old-fashioned coat with large cuffs awash with lace stood before him, "Max Calvert." The man moved his silver tankard from his right hand to the left with dexterity, losing only a whiff of spice from his Arrack punch.

Field stood and took the offered hand. "Should I know you, sir?"

Max Calvert cracked a wide, practiced smile. "I know your father from my years as alderman and mayor of this borough." Max sat down across from Archer and signaled for the coffee boy. "I heard you were staying with Mrs. Fleet." His eyes narrowed as if trying to catch Archer in a lie.

"Yes."

"These are dangerous times. Prudent men know where they stand and where their neighbors stand."

"Indeed, I have heard it said that there is wisdom in a multitude of counselors."

"Just so." Max drank deeply from his tankard.

Field ordered his coffee and the latest paper.

"We haven't had a new paper in weeks. Holt's *Gazette* was our only source. I assume you heard what happened."

Field nodded that he had. "What is your concern with Mrs. Fleet?"

The old eyes widened this time as if innocence was all they ever beheld. "I've known Delany Fleet since she and her father first came to work for old Thomas Fleet." He took another drink. "She is the same age as one of my daughters. Always was a good girl."

Satisfied that Calvert was not another Crawley, Field said, "She used to come with her father on buying trips to Archer Hall. I knew her then. I am to take her to her brother-in-law's as soon as the roads are passable."

"I am glad to hear it. I've removed my wife to Pomfret, and there she will stay for the duration of this mess. It is my good fortune that my daughters are married with husbands still alive to protect them."

"Calvert, I see you have met our Mrs. Fleet's house guest," John Crawley bellowed from behind Max Calvert, slapping him on the back as he reached the man.

"Indeed. Are you acquainted with Mr. Archer?" Calvert's eyes once again narrowed at Field.

Field raised an eyebrow. "We have met."

Crawley dropped the fake smile.

"Mr. Archer will escort Mrs. Fleet to her brother in Princess Anne." Calvert winked at Field before taking another draft from his tankard.

Crawley's eyes flashed. His face flushed. "She didn't mention that to me when I saw her just now."

"Perhaps she doesn't tell you everything, John. You're not her guardian." Calvert slid farther down the bench. "Stop hovering and sit down. You give me a crick in the neck."

Field had forgotten the forthrightness of the inhabitants of his native colony. In London, the conversation would hardly be so blunt. It was refreshing.

"I'll be about my business. See you watch yourself with Mrs. Fleet. She is not without friends." The threat in Crawley's eyes was unmistakable.

Calvert twisted his bulk to watch Crawley leave. Once Crawley was safely out of earshot, Calvert turned back to Field. "How did you make an enemy of John Crawley so quickly? My intelligence says you've been here less than a fortnight."

"I suspect he has a liking for Mrs. Fleet."

"Yes." Calvert drank again. "He's not as powerful as he thinks he is, but he can be a significant annoyance if he wants to be. One is never quite sure of all the shadows he might be hiding in."

"What do you mean, shadows?"

"To use an old phrase, he has his hands in a lot of pots."

"Why are you telling me all this?"

"For your father's sake, of course." He gave that practiced smile again. Calvert the politician had already decided who would win. "Lord Dunmore's a fool. He had the Scots merchants in his pocket before he came. He should have slowed down a little. Taken a breath and looked around. Instead, he came and threatened to free our servants. It'll backfire. Mark my words. He will come out of this the most hated man in Virginia. Ye can't force love or loyalty, my boy."

"I have heard of his Captain Squire plundering the

local plantations."

"He's not your worry. You have to watch out for the so-called 'commissioned' Tories who are nothing but criminals hanging about in the swamps." Calvert rose and went away with a wave of his hand.

Field left the coffee house after he'd finished his coffee. He was glad their journey had been postponed long enough to make preparations that he'd not anticipated. He would start with Ben.

6

"Mr. Field." Mary startled him. He'd been listening to the rain in the parlor next to the fireplace in his favorite chair absorbed in a book on agricultural advances. She'd been so quiet he hadn't realized she was there. "May I speak to you?"

"Of course, Mrs. Tabb. What is it?"

She sat down in the chair across from him. "I've heard some things, and I just wanted to know if you plan to tell your mother not to associate with Miss Delany anymore—not let Miss Delany sell her dolls."

Where had she come up with that? He had been thinking that his mother should refrain from the odd association, but he'd not confided that to anyone. Did he talk in his sleep? If he did, Mary Tabb would never know it.

"Miss Delany is the alonest person I ever knew and the kindest," Mary continued. "She takes care of herself, and she takes care of everyone else. She don't deserve that from you."

He couldn't answer that. Not yet.

She must have been about ten or eleven years old the first time he'd seen her. Her father, Jimmy Button, had come on Fleet's behalf to trade with his father.

What must it have been like to be indentured with her father? He'd never thought about it.

Jimmy Button was a shrewd but honest man. A good man. Field's father told him that Fleet had done well in his choice of servant.

How was it that someone he'd known for so long was still a mystery? An alluring mystery, at that.

Delany Button had one long braid down her back that day. He'd just been down to the rope room. Eyes wide with wonder and curiosity, she asked about the rope and how it was made. He'd learned since not to bore a woman like that, but at the time, he described everything he knew about growing hemp and making rope. When he was done, she still stood enraptured.

Delany was a remarkable woman. True, he hadn't made up his mind about her yet. She was so different from the child he'd known. Or maybe she wasn't. He didn't know, and he couldn't promise anything to Mary Tabb until he did. Delany Fleet was an alluring mystery, indeed.

"Tell me about Mr. Tom," he said.

Her look soured. "Not much worth telling about that man. He was the greediest soul I ever knew."

"How so?"

"Sometimes people are round, and sometimes they're flat. Mr. Tom was flat. All about money. How much he could make and how much he could sell so he could make more. Not like his brother, Mr. Samuel. Mr. Tom was flat and hard like a shilling."

"How did Miss Delany wind up married to him?"

"Some things it's not my place to tell, and that's

one of them." She smiled at him as if she'd thought of something new. "When Mr. Tom died, she was lost for a while. But I don't think it was about Mr. Tom. It was for her father. He'd died the same time the year before. She was all alone then. Mr. Tom was no kinda family to have, but he was what she had."

Heartache fatigued his chest. Thoughts of Archer Hall filled with his brothers and sister. Too much time since he'd been home.

"Are you gonna tell Miss Ann not to let Miss Delany sell her dolls?"

"No."

~*~

She'd forgotten how large a man he was. Field Archer filled the chair next to the unlit fireplace. In the week he had stayed with her, it had become his chosen seat. Delany found they all left it vacant so that he might be comfortable. He sat there now reading an agricultural journal by the light of a candle.

She had missed him. That truth was uncomfortable. Rambling walks with him crisscrossing the entire plantation stood out in her memories illuminated like the amber glow that now traced his hair. But then regret would stain the memory with shame that she'd ever entertained the hope that he would love her and make her his own. The sting of rejection had faded long ago, but the shame flamed bright again when accused by John Crawley. Had the old hope flared when she'd seen him again? She hadn't thought so, but John Crawley seemed to think that it had.

She couldn't afford to revert to her old fantasies. She would lose her dreams. Her only hope lay in facing her feelings straight on. Had she missed him? Yes. His presence in her house was no longer stifling, but that didn't mean she wanted him. She wanted freedom: freedom to make her own choices, freedom to choose her own destiny.

Construction was progressing nicely on Button Cove according to the last report she'd heard from Williams. Lord Dunmore's blockages had restricted the mail, so she hadn't heard from her foreman in three months. Perhaps she should consider traveling there after she'd dropped Ben at home. Soon she would sell her house and remove far away from the muddy streets teeming with horses and British soldiers, who could storm in and take up residence in any house they chose.

"What have you heard from London, Mrs. Fleet?" Archer's deep voice resonated in the room.

"Nothing more than I've heard from you. I'm sure you must have heard that Lord Dunmore has blockaded the entire town. The region, for that matter."

"I thought perhaps you got news from your ships."

"My ship arrived back in early September. And so she sits."

"Any damage from the hurricane?"

"Remarkably, no."

"I had lunch in The King's Arms today. I heard

Calvert is removing to Pomfret."

Delany's heart warmed at the thought of her old friends. "He's not the first one. I'm glad for Mrs. Calvert, but it's troubling to see our leaders absconding to safer domains."

"He told me that the swamps are teaming with ne'er-do-wells."

"Criminals that call themselves Tories are more like it."

"Raiding farms like proper British soldiers," Sarah added.

Field's face relaxed into a smile at Sarah's joke.

Delany couldn't remember the last time she'd seen him smile like that.

Ben's eyes grew round, and he sat up on the edge of his seat. "Do you think we'll have to kill 'em?"

Field lost the smile and took on a somber expression. He responded before Delany formed an answer. "I hope not. Killing a man is not a light thing."

"Have you ever killed anyone?" Anticipation animated Ben's entire body.

"No, and I hope I never will."

"My father says we have a duty and a right to protect our family." The phrase was an obvious quote from another conversation, most likely just like this one.

"Your father is right. We have to protect our families, but we don't go looking for trouble."

Ben deflated.

"But"–Field added with a grin—"we're not afraid if trouble finds us."

Field did sound like Samuel then.

Ben matched his grin and sat back in his seat a little more sedate.

7

Delany was walking up the cobbled path to her home when she heard musket fire. A plume of smoke rose from her garden and drifted her way. Stomach queasy, she ran to the garden gate.

Once inside, she found Ben and Archer in front of a wooden placard with a mark and a hole in it.

"Follow through is the thing— "

"What are you doing?" she demanded.

"Aunt Delany, look what Mr. Archer gave me." Ben's eyes gleamed with pride. It was a shiny new flintlock. No doubt where that came from.

She smiled at Ben and was rewarded with a quick embrace. He was excited.

"We are getting ready for our journey," Archer said.

"We must be prepared for anything that might happen, Aunt Delany." The grin disappeared from Ben's face, replaced with the manly seriousness he had been cultivating. Innocent brown eyes requested approval.

She nodded and turned toward the house.

Archer followed. "I suppose you are wondering what I am about, teaching your nephew these tactics."

"You are quite wrong, sir. I was wondering what took you so long to get started."

"Took so long?"

She turned to face him. "Mr. Archer, we have a serious journey ahead of us. Do you suppose I wish my nephew to be a ninny, unable to look after himself?"

"No. I–"

"I wish him to get to his parents alive. His chances significantly increase if he can take care of himself. When he is home, his father will see to such things. Until then, you will just have to do."

Field arched his eyebrows.

Delany headed into the house to seek a cup of tea to calm her shaking insides.

"Well done," Sarah said as she took Delany's work basket and placed it on a table.

"I know it's the right thing. It just worries me to put him in danger. What will I tell his parents if anything happens to him?"

"A man needs to stand on his own."

"Thirteen years old is not a man."

"I'll grant you that, but he never will be if he's coddled. I am glad he knows his way around a Brown Betty."

Delany smiled. "It's a Brown Bess."

"Oh, that's right," Sarah giggled, "Brown Betty is the apple crumble. Not sure why I get them confused."

"Let's just get some tea."

~*~

As Delany took the last bite of her apple crumble, she caught the eye of her nephew. "Ben, after supper, I should like you to join me in the garden with your Bess."

Trepidation pinched his features.

"It's been a few years since I used my father's squirrel gun, and I should like you to refresh my memory."

Trepidation swelled to pride.

"Yes, Aunt. We can go now if you'd like,"—he shoved the last bite of dessert into his mouth and added—"while there's still plenty of light."

Once in the garden, Ben proceeded to show Delany all the parts of his new gun. His thirteen-year-old impatience was stilled. Methodically he showed her step by step how to load the powder, pack the ball, and prime the pan. She bit back the urge to compete with his knowledge with "I know, yes, I know." Her reward was a clearer window into the man he would become.

"Now," he said, "if you could hold this." He handed her the loaded rifle. It was a good deal longer and heavier than her father's squirrel gun. "Point it this way so no one gets hurt." He shoved the barrel toward the ground. Some powder sprinkled to the ground from the pan. "That's all right. It's better to be safe." He walked over to the tree and hung the placard on a nail. When he returned to her side, she handed the loaded rifle back to him. He re-primed the pan.

"You hold it like this." He demonstrated by raising the gun into a firing position on his shoulder and squinted down the barrel. "You line up your shot and gently pull the trigger." When he fired, he hit his mark.

Delany clapped. "Excellent!"

He glowed. "Now you do it." He handed the musket to her.

Delany powdered, packed, and primed the pan. She hefted the rifle to her shoulder and took aim.

"Line up the shot."

Her gaze danced off the target at the sound of Field's quiet voice. She didn't move. She forced herself to look down the barrel of the rifle.

"Take a deep breath," he instructed, "Now gently squeeze." His body, rock solid behind her, warmed her back.

The stock jammed into her shoulder. Smoke clouded her vision. She couldn't see the target. She stepped away from the smoke to see her shot. She was off the mark, but she still hit the piece of wood. Maybe she wasn't as rusty as she'd thought. She didn't want to be embarrassed in front of Field Archer ever again. She'd had enough of that for one lifetime.

"You were too fast, Aunt Delany."

Her face flamed hot. "What do you mean? I hit the board. That's pretty good."

"He's talking about follow through." Field said, "You moved too quickly after you fired."

Delany started to reload the rifle. *I can do this. It was just heavier and longer than I was used to—that's all.* When she was ready, she lifted the long gun once more and moved her feet into position. She lined up her shot when Field placed his hands on her waist. She froze.

"With your permission." He changed her body's angle to the target.

Delany jerked a slight nod and widened her arms to try to get him to move his hands. He slid his arms once again into place. *Does he know what he is doing to me? Never happen.* She took a deep breath and forced her gaze to focus on the sights. Breathe out.

Fire. Huge blinding smoke.

"Hold," he said and tightened his grip on her waist. "Give it time." He released her as the smoke thinned.

She abruptly moved away.

"You did it!" Ben cheered.

She had hit her mark. "Thank you." She bowed to Field. "I think I can take it from here."

He clasped his hands behind his back. "It was my pleasure."

"The rest is just practice. Right, Mr. Archer?" Ben asked.

"Right."

"Right," Delany echoed.

They stood for an awkward moment looking at each other.

She smiled at them both. "Now go away so I can practice."

~*~

The night was cool for early October. Leaves rustled just outside the open window near Field's chair by the fireplace. A steady breeze riffled the curtain and chilled his arm. Soon it would be time for brilliant roaring fires that sent warm glows across the parlor, making cheery rooms that otherwise would be somber. Tonight, there was only a watered-down version of the blaze he envisioned. There were plenty of candles, but the shadows cast were deep, anxiety-ridden hollows. At home, there were so many occupants that tense silence was never achieved.

Delany worked her needle as she sat next to Mrs. Harrison on the couch.

Mrs. Harrison knitted.

"You know tales are still told by the ancient ones of dead men walking on All Hallow's Eve," he said to Ben.

Ben sat up from his slouch in the chair. "What ancient ones?"

"The old ones I met in my travels in Ireland and Scotland."

Delany chortled.

"You've heard stories of Grace from the swamp, not that I believe in that sort of thing," said Mrs. Harrison without looking up from her needles.

"Do you think witches are real?" Ben asked.

Delany looked at Field. "Yes," she answered.

Was she serious?

As scientific as he found her, a woman who owned a waterfall believed in ancient superstitions?

Delany leaned toward Ben. "Did your father ever tell you of the time when we were children of the fright we gave to Old Cook?"

"No." Ben's eyes widened.

Delany laughed, her cloth resting in her lap. "I don't suppose he would." She leaned forward, eyes sparkling in the candlelight. "Old Cook told us tales to keep us from the new fairy cakes she made. 'The fairies'll come', she said, 'and take ya to the fairy mound, and you'll never come back from there. None ever does.'"

Ben laughed at Delany's mimic of the old woman.

Field had to laugh with him.

"Well, that was enough for us. No cakes," she continued. "Until later that night, Uncle Tom and Samuel heard her telling John Milkman what she'd done while he enjoyed a few of her fresh cakes. They had a right jolly laugh, Uncle Tom said." Delany folded her cloth into a proper square. "Your father, Uncle Tom, and I made a plan. It was mostly Uncle Tom, but your father and I went right along with it." She looked at Field, her silver eyes twinkling. "To raise the specter of Grace Sherwood."

A small shiver of wind tickled the back of Field's neck.

"Late one night, when it was storming—not calm like tonight—there were flashes of lightning streaking through the room. We dressed up Sam—he was the tallest—a bit of the moss and an old dress." She stopped to giggle. "He was the best hag I've ever seen."

Field sat back with a smile on his face.

Ben was on the edge of his seat.

Mrs. Harrison's needles lay quiet.

"We crept quietly up the stairs," Delany

whispered, "to her room. Sam threw the door open wide. There was Cook sitting with her candle. The scream she let out nearly put us in the stocks." She laughed. "We were most fortunate the dear lady didn't die that night."

Field's laugh mingled with Ben's and Mrs. Harrison's. He hadn't seen such delight on Delany's face since he'd showed her the dandelion in the field all those years ago. It had been her last visit to Archer Hall. He had missed her. He used to wonder why she hadn't come back, but then he'd heard that she'd married Tom Fleet.

"So, you do believe that witches are real?" he asked.

"The Bible says they are," she responded, "but I'm not sure that people always identify them correctly."

"Have you ever met one?" Ben piped up.

"I don't know. I know the Word says they are real, but God has not shown any to me."

"It's a most unscientific position to hold in these enlightened times, Mrs. Fleet. Current thinking says there is no such thing as ghosts or witches. It's all a humbug easily explained by facts."

"Science professes to know a great many things. It has yet to explain why. It understands how, but it doesn't know why. Why is the candle flickering here present on your face? Why?"

"I will agree that science doesn't have all the answers yet."

"Do you believe in angels, Mr. Archer?"

"Yes, of course. Numerous examples are present in

our readings every Sunday."

"Then you should have no trouble with their counterparts."

She rose.

He stood and bowed.

~*~

This sparring with him was too comfortable. Delany climbed the stairs to her room. Her heart softened at his laughter; her body thrilled to his touch. It was time to be out of his presence while she was still safe. For all John Crawley's faults, he was right on one score: Field Archer would never love a servant, no matter how different her life had become.

8

Field sat astride his horse waiting while Delany, list in hand, checked and double-checked each and every box. She tested the ropes securing the wagon. Field's cargo was hidden in plain sight amongst the boxes labeled "Fleets Toys and Curiosities" and other distinguishable household items including a couple of old chairs and a cupboard. She had done a brilliant job. Her wagon looked no different than the steady stream of wagons that had been leaving Norfolk down Church Street since he'd arrived.

He waited while she checked that every person was in place with everything they might possibly need. Ruben Tabb sat in the driver's seat of the cargo wagon. Mrs. Harrison, her maid Sally, and Mary Tabb were in the coach. Joe Wheelwright stood next to the door of the coach patiently waiting to secure the steps once she entered. Ben sat on his horse, clearly as itchy to leave as Field was himself.

"Mrs. Fleet."

She paused to look back at him and stuck a finger in the air. "Just one more thing, Mr. Archer." She rushed up the steps back into the house. She returned forthwith carrying a tea chest which she stowed somewhere in the coach. One more pull at the house door to ensure its locked state and one more look around at her arrangements until she finally mounted the steps of the coach.

Joe pulled up the stairs, and they began to walk away from Norfolk.

Field took the lead with Ben at his side. The coach followed with the wagon of goods bringing up the rear. It had been a week since he'd met Max Calvert at the coffee house and been warned of the thieving, murderous bands of Tories infesting the swamps around Princess Anne. If he could just get his cargo past this road, he would be in the clear. A week was not quite enough time, but he had done what he could with it. Ben already knew his way around a musket before Field had arrived but had grown rusty living in the city. He was well practiced now. Field was confident that Ben would survive whatever they encountered.

The roads were soft but passable provided they went slowly and avoided the crusted ruts left by those willing to travel in the mud that had delayed them for the past two weeks.

The sun baked his back the two hours it took to leave Norfolk behind. Once out of the city, they entered a dappled shade provided by closely growing trees lining both sides of the road. The fall colors of the tall sweet gums, maples, and oaks shamed the stained glass of cathedrals he'd seen in Europe. A freshening breeze swiftly dusted through the branches. His mouth watered when he saw a bush of chokeberries in the woods almost within reach. He took a deep breath. It was good to be on Virginia soil again.

Chokeberries. He smiled to himself. He hadn't seen a chokeberry in years. Hadn't grown so much as a potted plant since he'd been in England.

It was faint. The wind was not quite in the right direction, but it was unmistakable.

Walls of trees contained the sounds of the wagons and the horses blunting Field's ability to sense the landscape surrounding them, but the sound of a single man riding a horse was as clear as a weed in a well-tended garden.

"Good day to you, sir," the man said as he pulled up on Field's right side. Ben stayed on his left. "It's a fine day to travel." This man was not the source of the smell he'd detected as they'd approached the bend in the road. Someone else, at least one man, was still nearby.

The man in sight was large and finely dressed. Though wearing his own hair, this man gave every impression of being a Virginia gentleman. And one could hardly fault a man for wearing his own hair in the Virginia heat. He himself was guilty of the same since he'd been home.

"Yes, it is indeed," Field responded. He put his hand down toward his flintlock.

"That won't be necessary, sir. I mean you no harm. I am merely traveling this road on the way to Great Bridge."

Sounds of two more riders joining them assaulted his ears.

The coach stopped.

Field put out his left hand to signal Ben to stop. Field stopped. The man wheeled around to look at the coach.

"Josiah Philips. I thought that was you." Delany stood on the doorway of her coach with a flintlock aimed at the stranger. "You and your men leave right now, or your wife will have a bad day."

Philips pointed a pistol at Ben.

"Mrs. Fleet." He smiled wide. "I don't want anything from you. I only want Mr. Archer for Lord Dunmore."

Delany didn't move.

Philips nodded at his men. They walked their way forward to meet him. "Lord Dunmore will be disappointed that I didn't bring Mr. Archer. I hate to tell him that you kept me from doing my duty, Mrs. Fleet."

The smell of evil rolling off Josiah Philips nearly choked him now.

Ashen faced, her silver eyes met his.

Field nodded.

"Good girl." Philips grinned.

Delany's eyes flashed.

"Enough." Field smiled at Delany and nodded. "Until we meet again, Mrs. Fleet."

Philips requested and received Field's musket. Using the pistol, he pointed Field to get in front of him. The men flanked him on either side, and they took off at a trot.

~*~

Delany jumped down from the coach and headed toward Ben. The boy sat rigid in his saddle, head darting this way and that, mind clearly racing.

"Ben."

"I'll follow them. I'll meet you at the inn."

"No." She caught the reins just as he made to turn. "Get down. You have to go for help."

"But—"

The look she gave him silenced him, and he reluctantly slid down from the saddle.

"I know these woods," she said. "You go in the coach and get your father."

"You can't mean to go by yourself, Miss Delany," Joe said from his perch atop the coach.

"You and Ruben continue on to Fleet's. Samuel will know where I am."

She climbed onto Ben's horse thankful for her brown traveling skirts. They would help conceal her in the woods until Samuel could arrive to help.

~*~

Field prayed that Philips hadn't heard the snap of Ben's horse running parallel to them in the woods. Then he prayed that Delany would have the good sense to send her brother-in-law and not herself in pursuit.

Hopefully, she would have seen to the rifles, but he doubted it. She wasn't very good at taking directions, especially from him. He nearly smiled at the thought of her pulling away from him as he repositioned her firing stance. The fire of her silver eyes when Philips said "good girl" had been priceless.

"Go get the boy," Philips said to the henchman on his left.

"He's just a child. He can't harm you," Field said.

"You ever watch anyone die, Archer?"

Field shot him a look.

Philips grinned.

"It's a struggle. People want to live, you see." Malevolence emblazed his eyes. "Better than any brew."

Field's intellectual doubt of the personification of evil died. A shaft of fear cooled his anger. This was evil in a human wrapper. His mind cleared. There had to be a way out, and he would find it.

"What do you want?"

"Money."

"That can be arranged. Provided no harm comes to him."

"Not so fast. I haven't talked to Mrs. Fleet yet. He's worth more to her, I reckon. And then there's that family of his over at Lynnhaven."

The grimy man returned in a gallop.

"I didn't find nobody."

Field kept track of the turns in direction by keeping track of the waning sun. By evening, he was reasonably sure he could find his way back to the road. How he would escape his captors was not readily clear.

They came to rest at a well-used camp in a clearing surrounded by murky swamp and Spanish-moss laden trees. He dismounted on spongy legs.

The two men with Philips dismounted as well but didn't seem to have the stiff-legged problem.

Philips stayed on his horse.

"Where you think you're going?" the smelly one demanded.

"Nature's call," Field said dragging his ill functioning legs toward the trees.

Philips gestured, and the putrid man followed a few steps behind. He remained next to the tree while Field surveyed the ground before him. Philips still sat astride when Field returned to the clearing.

"I regret that I may not remain with you for the entire evening. I have other appointments which will not keep," Philips said. "I will return in the morning. Then we shall see what Lord Dunmore would have us do with you." Philips's smile was like an etching of the devil Archer had seen in a picture-book somewhere.

Field suppressed a shudder and nodded an unnecessary reply.

"Keep him here until I return," Philips ordered his men.

At least he was leaving. They would have to sleep sometime.

~*~

Field's nether regions were stiff from sitting on a log by the campfire. While the fire roasted his cheeks, the nighttime breeze cooled his back. Philips had been gone for at least three hours. Field had until daylight. Night had fallen, and the men guarding him were becoming tired and lazy.

They had ridden for two hours before stopping at this clearing. Obviously, it was a camp frequented by this bunch. If he'd kept himself oriented correctly, the road lay off to his right. If he could get there, he was certain he could make it to the inn. From there, he would travel to the Fleets' home.

The flames in the small fire blazed higher when one of the men threw a pulpy log in its midst.

The woods beyond were his escape route. The moon was rising, and soon stars would be visible. He could find his way. He wasn't sure he saw it at first. A figure, indistinct in the light, hovered near the woods.

"Did you see that?" the smelly man asked, his pale face blanching in the fire's glow.

"What?"

"That." The man's hand shook as he pointed to the flames.

"I don't see nothin'."

"It's Grace." Both men stood peering through the fire at the woods. "My old mother said she roams around here."

"You spooked. She's been dead for years."

"They say her body vanished when she died."

"Don't nobody knows what happened when she died."

A shuffle of leaves. Snap of a small twig.

"Didja hear that?"

"So."

"Sounds like a cat. She always had black cats."

"Too heavy for a cat."

Wintery fingers tickled his neck. "If angels are real, demons are, too," he said softly.

"Shut up!" the second man snapped.

Another shuffling in the woods sounded to the right.

Both men pointed their guns at the sound.

Across the clearing, Field saw a small, gaunt specter materialize in front of a large oak fifty yards from the fire, dragged up from the depth of the earth like Samuel. Streaks of grime, scrapings of the passage up through layers of swamp, oozed down from its hair to its skirts. A ragged dress hung from its frame without the fullness of undergarments. White flesh, luminescent in the light of the fire, glowed through tears in mud-slicked sleeves. It took a ragged step forward.

A breath of cold shivered around him. Field froze. His captors stopped moving. He didn't dare take his attention from the specter before them to gauge what they were doing.

Slowly, it raised its arms. Tattered bits of flesh landed just behind it as it moved slowly forward. Its face cracked, the flesh crumbling before them as it beckoned. A horrid black ring where its mouth should be formed a word. "Come," it appeared to say. "Come…"

It drew closer.

"Come," it beckoned. "Come."

The men turned and ran into the woods behind

them.

Field ran toward the apparition. He scooped her up and threw her over his shoulder and made it to the woods before he stopped to check for followers.

"Where's the horse?"

"Put me down," she demanded in a low growl.

He obliged her because they needed the horse and she couldn't very well give him directions upside down with nothing but the ground to navigate by.

She had left the horse a half mile away. They covered the ground in slow motion.

He climbed onto the horse and pulled Delany up in front of him. She slid her blunderbuss around to sit on her lap.

Field reached for the musket stowed in the saddle. No surprises this time. Shoot first. He turned toward the road.

She had saved him. When he had a few minutes, he would have to think about what that meant. Right now, he was glad to feel her slight but solid, dirty form in his arms. A stiff tendril scratched his nose and made his eyes water.

"What is that in your hair?" Even mud streaks couldn't coarsen the softness of the auburn curls that twined about his fingers as he attempted to brush out any further hindrances to his eyesight.

"Moss."

"You could've gotten killed."

"I was armed. You could've gotten killed."

"You should've sent Samuel."

"You couldn't wait that long."

9

Delany had thought that the first time she was in his arms they would be face to face dancing, not riding a horse in the dark of night while she was covered in swamp dirt. She sat up straight trying to maintain distance between them. The warmth of his body enticed her to relax into its comfort. To fit her back to his contours would soothe her bones, like a roaring fire warmed her scalp by filling strands of her hair with heat as it dried. Mud and moss had transformed her into a witch of the Dismal Swamp. Now she would have to pay the price. Wet through, Delany was beginning to freeze. Deep in her belly, shivers began to shudder through her limbs. What she would give to be in Molly Fleet's kitchen in front of its large stone fireplace or sitting in a tub filled with hot water washing off the grime that was slowing drying into a tight skin.

Field slid his free arm around her waist and tugged her flat against his body. Heat surrounded her. She wriggled to create an inch or two between them and still retain his radiance.

"Be still." His baritone slipped down her ear and quieted her protest as he covered her with the flaps of his coat. After half a mile of steady running while being held in his arms, her convulsions quieted to mere ripples and faded. Another half a mile, and they had cleared the woods and started down the road toward the twin bridges. Once they cleared the bridges, they would be in Molly's kitchen within no more than an hour and a half, assuming, of course, that Josiah Philips had not heard of Field's escape.

~*~

It wasn't until he could see the glistening river that Field realized how far they had traveled. The first of two bridges lay in front of them. His impulse was to risk the noise and bound over them. Instead, he slowed. The moon was high. Tiny fists of clouds still shivered in its cold light and had not coalesced into a bank to cover them as they walked across the exposed bridge.

A black man as tall as the withers of the draft they were riding came out of the woods waving his hands above his head. Delany recoiled into his chest before resuming her stiffened back. Field took hold of Delany's blunderbuss and pointed it at the man, hand on the trigger.

"Miss Delany? That you in there?" the man called out in a coarse whisper.

Delany put her hand on Field's and lowered the gun as she peered out around the collar of his great coat. "Wiley?"

The man let out a breath and raised his face to the

sky. "Thank You, Jesus." Turning back to them he said, "Miss Delany, Mr. Samuel told me you was in trouble. I guess he reckoned I would come and find you while he took care of the folks that's showed up at his place."

"Wiley," Delany separated herself from Field and sat forward in the saddle.

Field resumed control of the gun.

"Thank God, you've come." She reached out for Wiley's hand. When he took it, she continued. "We've got to get to Samuel's."

"Shhhh." Wiley put a finger to his lips. "Miss Delany, there's bad folks out tonight. I seent them down on the river." He pointed toward the bridge. "Come with me." He pointed to the copse of trees just before the small clearing that led to the bridge.

Still mounted, hand on the trigger, Field directed the horse to follow Wiley into the darkness under the trees.

"Why do you trust this man?" he whispered.

"Because he's my friend," she whispered back.

"More than that," Wiley answered. "But that's a story for another day. I will always come for Miss Delany." Wiley reached for a sack sitting on the ground. "Now, we got to still those hoofs."

Delany moved to dismount.

Field held her in place.

She turned to face him in the saddle. He couldn't see the flash in her silver eyes in the darkness, but he could feel the challenge. She pulled her blunderbuss out of his grasp. "What choice do you have?" Her breath slid across his lips. A stray piece of moss scraped across his face as she slid down the saddle to the ground. He pulled the rifle out of the saddle sheath and dismounted.

Wiley sorted through a pile of rags he had pulled from the sack.

Delany reached for one and headed for a leg.

A series of whistles pierced the trees.

Delany and Wiley froze.

Field barely breathed.

Boats thumped. Oars clattered. Muffled curses were too far away to be distinguishable on this branch of the river.

He resumed breathing and stepped out from the trees headed toward the tall grasses leaning over the river bank. The bridge lay fifty feet in front of them at the end of the road. Morris's Inn sat dark on the stump of land perched between the two branches of the river. The carriage yard lay shadow-less in the moonlight. The men down below began to shout at each other. He recognized Josiah Philips. Still too far away to hear exactly what was said, the timbre of the voice was unmistakable.

They would have to go quickly.

Field returned to the trees to find the hooves had been wrapped.

Delany had transformed herself again, her hair tied up in a kerchief, no doubt from Wiley's bag. Face still pale from dried mud, she was a different woman.

Wiley stuffed the remaining rags into his sack. He took his position at the horse's head on the right. He motioned to Field to stay on the right side. Delany climbed up and threw herself across the saddle on her stomach.

Delany dead. Even the pretense made him downright uncomfortable. He'd felt better after he'd actually been punched in the gut. It was a good disguise, but he was not fooled. In this light, Delany didn't look like a dead slave. The curve of her neck was too supple. The turn of her elbow too delicate.

"No one will believe this twice in the same night."

She angled up to face him and said, "They will."

Her certainty astounded him.

"They shan't. It's too preposterous."

"People believe all sorts of preposterous things, Field Archer."

"I cannot let you—shall not let you—go through with this. We don't know who that is down there."

"What—"

"I don't want to hear 'what choice do you have?'"

She sat up in the saddle, silver eyes blazing.

"Turn around, legs to that side," he pointed to the side most visible to the men on the river. She grinned at him before she rotated and hung down once again. How could she possibly enjoy herself? They could all be killed.

The mud caked on her dangling limbs helped. Field prayed it would be enough. There were at least ten men down there, and evil rowed with them.

He searched the saddle for Ben's powder and shot bag and placed them in his coat. Holding the rifle in parallel with his left leg, he was ready.

Wiley rounded his tall height and shoulders into

submission.

They walked to the bridge.

Field paced his steps with Wiley. Fifteen steps took them to the inn yard. They moved swiftly across the yard toward the second bridge. The shouts got louder. A pistol cracked. The horse snuffled and took a step back.

"Whatchu doin' there, boy?" a voice yelled from below.

Wiley kept his head down and kept walking.

"Keep your eyes on what you're doing," Philips' voice menaced. "He's carrying his dead."

Field itched to peek down the river but didn't dare risk Delany's exposure. He caught a tremor out of the corner of his eye. She was beginning to shiver. He took her hand. She grabbed on and held hard. Field let out the breath he'd been holding once his feet reached the sandy bank of the road.

"I thought that might be you, Mrs. Fleet." Josiah Philips stood on the road. Alone this time, hands in his pockets. "Mr. Archer." He nodded his head.

Field looked down the sights of his rifle and moved to stand in front of the horse.

"Move now."

"No need to be so hostile, Mr. Archer. I'll not detain you again this evening. As you can see, I am occupied with my own affairs at the moment." Philips gestured toward the river.

Field didn't flinch.

"I merely came up so that you wouldn't think I was quite so stupid as to think that the beautiful Mrs.

Fleet was a slave." His face coiled into a grin. "My men might be fanciful, but I'm not." He stood aside with a wave of his arm to let them pass.

Field kept his rifle aimed at Philips as they passed but couldn't stop the ball that flew from Philips pistol into Wiley. Field returned fire, but Philips slipped into the woods.

Wiley began to run, pulling the horse along with him. Blood was running from the wound in his shoulder.

They ran at least a mile before they stopped.

Delany slid off of the horse.

Wiley shook his head.

"Don't argue with me, Wiley," Delany commanded.

"It don't hurt that bad, Ms. Delany." He looked at Field for support.

"What choice do you have?" Field responded.

Wiley climbed up into the saddle.

"You get up there, too." Field ordered.

"No. I'm freezing, and a little walk will do me good."

He couldn't argue with that. The night was getting even colder.

10

The lights in Molly's kitchen and house sang peace into the night. The moon silvered the tall birches in the yard.

Delany stumbled in relief as she approached the house. Her spirit whispered, *home.*

"They're here!" Ben's voice carried out to her, and her eyes filled with tears. Ben was here in the warmth and care of his parents. He was safe. She wiped the tear that fell when the door opened, and Ben ran down the steps.

Sarah banged the door back open when Ben dropped it, and Samuel and Molly came out right behind her.

"Aunt Delany!" He collided with her and folded her into his arms. *Home.* He stepped back and took a look. "You're crunchy. Did you fall into the swamp?"

"I'm filthy. You better tell Mary to make up a tub."

"Mary's in bed. I'll tell Betsy."

"No. Tell Betsy to come here. I've another job for her."

He ran back to the house.

Delany turned back to Wiley and Archer.

Wiley had dismounted and stood without

assistance holding his shoulder.

"Freewill." A tiny black woman stood at the door of the kitchen peering into the darkness. "Freewill, is that you?"

"Betsy." The call in his voice was for none but her.

She flew down the porch to his side.

"I'm hurt."

She reached up to the tall man and held him in her arms. "Come with me."

They walked into the house moved by the love between them.

Delany was mesmerized by the feeling that she had come home.

Molly reached out and took Delany's hand. Sarah took the other one.

"Your hands are like stones. Let's get you inside." Molly rubbed Delany's fingers with her own warm hands.

"Did she just call him Freewill?"

~*~

Field creaked into the dining room behind Samuel. He didn't know when he'd been this tired or sore. Blisters the size of shillings were rising on his heels.

A large cherry wood table sat in the center of the room laden with platters of cold chicken, beef, and ham, a plate of bread, and a large bowl of apples. It was all he could do to keep his hand out of the bread plate and sit down in the seat offered. Across the table, in front of a small fireplace, sat Mrs. Harrison.

"Please, help yourself." Molly stood to hand him a plate from a stack sitting on the sideboard. "You must be famished."

"I hadn't realized how hungry I was until I entered this room." He was astonished that this was the truth. The last time he had thought of food was the tempting chokeberries by the side of the woods this morning. What a day. He helped himself to ham, beef, and a thick slice of bread. Robert brought a tumbler of dandelion tea. How appropriate. His favorite flower here to welcome him back from the most singular episode in his life to date. He silently said thanks to the Lord for sending Delany and for the dandelion tea.

Midway through his second mouthful of beef, beef that Mary would have a hard time besting, Delany entered the room. She was covered from throat to toe in a dressing gown of lavender trimmed in white lace. Her auburn hair, released from its knot and swamp debris, shimmered in the candlelight.

A remarkable woman. He had not seen her like in all his travels. Riding together left an imprint of her small frame in the circle of his embrace. How could so small a person in stature be brave enough to come after him when faced with an adversary as evil as Josiah Philips?

"Delany, sit by the fire." Molly directed from her seat next to her husband.

Mrs. Harrison tapped the seat cushion next to herself.

Delany shuffled to the offered seat directly across from him, her back to the fire. She looked at him and gave a sleepy smile that said, "We made it."

He smiled back. *We did.*

Five minutes later, a bandaged Wiley came in with Betsy. They took seats at the foot of the table.

Field passed the meat. Delany cast her sharp silver eyes at him with a question in their depths. Irritation rose. Did she think that he didn't know how to repay a debt of honor? In life, exceptions were always in order. Wiley had saved his life. More to the point, he had saved Delany's life. For that he would sit and eat with the man anywhere, anytime.

"Tell us what happened out there," Samuel said after the plates had been emptied the first time.

Delany related the events of the day in her straightforward way. The light twinkled in her hair jumping from tendril to tendril. Her eyes sparkled as she related the tale of the appearance of the Witch of Pungo.

Samuel laughed at her telling.

She was still laughing when she told of their harrowing escape across the bridge.

"It was hardly a laughing matter." the admonishment came unbidden from Field's mouth.

"It was our great escape," she teased. Her eyes flashed a silver challenge.

"You could have been killed. Wiley was shot."

Wiley looked up from his plate.

"It was a miracle of deliverance as sure as we are sitting around this table." Her smile disappeared as she drummed the table with her finger. "The joy I feel when a prayer is answered is no laughing matter, Mr.

Archer."

"If it was a miracle, and I am not ready to debate the question"—he took a breath—"miracles are not to be declared or treated flippantly, Mrs. Fleet."

She quieted, but he knew she wasn't done. Not if what blossomed her cheeks was anger. The past two weeks had taught him something of Delany Fleet. He was confident that it wasn't embarrassment. He grinned at her and turned to Samuel. "How long has smuggling been going on down at Moore's?"

"Probably since there's been a colony," Samuel responded from a relaxed position at the head of the table.

Samuel looked like his brother Tom, but so far, he appeared a very different type of man. The word Field used to describe Tom was hungry. Hungry for wealth. Hungry for power. Hungry for what he didn't have. Grasping. His brother was intelligent, confident, content. Sure of his place and content with it.

"It was Josiah Philips," Wiley injected from the end of the table.

"So now we know for sure," Samuel said as he sat up straight and leaned his elbows on the table. "We've known about smuggling down there for years. But it's been intermittent. Lately there's been an increase in activity. We weren't sure who was behind it."

"Philips?" Field asked.

"If that's who you saw, then that's who it is." Samuel took a sip from his glass. "I think there's more to it. Philips is a bad man, but he doesn't have the ability to plan like that."

"Someone else, then."

"Someone else directing and planning. I think so."

11

Delany awoke in her brother-in-law's house without the faintest idea of how she got to bed. Peace infused the house. She snuggled down in the covers and let the warm glow hug her heart hard. She would need it for the days ahead.

They had gotten this far. Ben was safe at home. Sarah's son would come and get her today. Then she and Field would set off for Williamsburg to deliver the rifles. The sight of Field captured by the fire in the clearing swept across her vision. She'd never been so scared in all her life and never so sure that she was doing the right thing, except for freeing Wiley and George. She glowed a deep thank you up to the Lord rather than say the words in a prayer. She felt His peace in response.

Delany threw back the covers and swung her feet onto the cold floor. The leaves on the maple tree outside her window were fringed in yellow and red.

Home. She never thought of Fleet farm as home. It was the home of her indenture when she visited as a girl. She'd lived most of her life in Norfolk. It wasn't clear when her father's dream of a farm in Northumberland had become her own dream.

Arriving last night to the glow of the kitchen and the arms of Molly and Ben hit her hard. The feeling of arriving home was unique. She had never felt it before. Not even returning to the Norfolk house after a long sales trip. *What does it mean, Lord? Please make it plain so I may walk the right path.*

Tom's house. She hadn't ever given it much thought. Thomas Fleet, her father-in-law, had built two houses at Fleet farm: one for each of his sons. Built just a mile and a half apart, Tom's house was the same as Samuel's. It didn't suit Tom to be so far from the city. "Too far from the action," he'd say. Samuel and Molly used it as a guest house when their house was full. They had plenty of room to accommodate their current company. Most likely Tom's house was empty. Tom's house.

Well, it was her house now, and she was within her rights to move into it if she chose. She'd never chosen to do so, preferring to stay in town and make money to fulfill her dream of moving to Northumberland. The possibility had never occurred to her before that she could stay in Princess Anne and sell her property in Norfolk. If she did that, she could forgo the expense of Northumberland. The acreage around Tom's house was more than what she needed.

A soft knock on the door had her padding toward her robe.

"Come in," she told Sally when she opened the door.

"Miss Delany," Sally bobbed a curtsey, "Miss Sarah said I should come help you as Mary is poorly this morning."

"Where is she?"

Delany followed Sally down the hall and up the stairs to the third floor.

"Mary?"

Mary struggled to sit up around the baby growing in her midsection. "What do you need, Miss Delany?"

Delany stepped over to the bed, "Nothing. Lie down," she said in her command voice, but softly. After Mary complied, Delany sat on the edge of the bed. "How are you feeling?"

"It's more than the buggy ride. You know, I never do like to ride in a buggy." She huffed and waved her hand. "Miss Molly's doctor says I have to stay put until the baby comes. He thinks it could be anytime now." Mary's eyes filled with tears. "It's too early, Miss Delany." She choked as the tears brimmed and fell down her cheeks.

Delany grabbed her hand. Mary pulled herself up, and Delany wrapped her in a tight hug.

"I'm glad you're here. I was so afraid for you."

"I was so afraid for Mr. Field I didn't take any time to be afraid for myself."

Mary grinned mischievously. "It's not too late for you. We all have to wait on the Lord's timing."

Delany nodded. It was never too late for the Lord to work a miracle. Mary needed a miracle. By their reckoning, the baby wasn't due for another couple of weeks. "It's time to pray, Mary."

They rocked, and they prayed, and they sang a song of praise.

"It'll be his timing, Mary."

"You won't leave me, will you?" Mary pleaded. Twenty-two years old, five years younger than Delany, standing on the brink of a terrifying unknown chasm that must be crossed. It didn't matter that thousands of women crossed the chasm before. Mary herself had not done it, and until she actually crossed the divide, she would have no peace.

"Of course I will stay with you. Don't you worry, now. Lie down and do exactly what the doctor says. We don't want little Ruben born before his time." She smiled.

Mary gave a bright smile back despite her tears.

Delany would tell Field that they would need to delay their departure for a few days. The dining room was empty when she arrived. Not surprising at ten o'clock. She headed for the kitchen. Betsy would have something she could eat, and she could find out about Wiley's new name. Outside she took a deep breath of the autumn air. It was always cooler out in the country. Norfolk never seemed to lose its stuffiness until the damp winters numbed one's bones. How had she stood it for so many years?

"Miss Delany!" Lucy Harrison barreled into her legs.

"Lucy!" Delany bent down and picked up the four-year old and clasped her tightly. "It's good to see you and Susan again." Delany never saw Lucy without her doll. If not clutched in her arms, Susan was always within a few feet. Susan was one of Ann Archer's gems. Flaxen-hair, dyed brown with startling blue eyes. The two could have been sisters.

"Me and Papa came to get Grams."

"Delany," Sarah, out of breath, arrived at her side. "You remember my son Isaac."

"Mr. Harrison. Nice to see you again."

Isaac Harrison was tall and browned by farming, his dark hair pulled back in a curlew at his neck. Blue eyes the color of West Indies color plates pierced everything they looked at even when crinkling a welcome as they did now. "Lucy couldn't talk of anything else once she knew you would be here with her Grams."

Delany looked down at the child. "Would you like to see what I brought you?"

The same blue eyes looked out of the small face with a big grin and a sprinkle of freckles. "Yes!"

Delany put Lucy down, and they walked toward the house hand in hand. Was this what the Lord meant by *home*? Isaac Harrison and a child of her own?

"I can do it myself." Lucy pulled her hand free and sidestepped to the right. "I can just walk with you."

"Yes, you can."

Lucy stood next to Delany's trunk, fingers on the edge, eyes wide. "What you got in that?"

Delany reached down into the corner and pulled out a small bundle wrapped in cloth tied with a purple ribbon.

"Oh, it's purple." Lucy took the package and crushed it to her chest. "My favorite color is purple."

Delany glowed. "Open it."

Inside, Delany had placed an elegant riding habit

of purple wool. "Susan is now ready to travel in high fashion."

"It's purple, too." Delany helped Lucy dress Susan in the tiny purple outfit.

~*~

Archer's breathing matched the rhythm of the canter as he pushed the stallion forward. Muscles hardened. Strength surged. Galloping hooves echoed his heartbeat. The smell of the Atlantic on the cool wind filled his mouth with every intake of breath.

It would never happen again. He'd been captive for mere hours, but he vowed it would never happen again. The lack of power for just those hours was all he needed. His gaze searched and found his firelock. He wouldn't be without it again, and Lord help him if he ever came across Josiah Philips.

The cleansing exercise brought him peace. Once he reached it, he stopped the horse and dismounted to rest them both. The sun had been up for about an hour. He needed to start back. Delany would be up soon. They needed to talk.

Lord Dunmore knew he was here. That put the entire Fleet family at risk. Field couldn't allow that any longer than the one night he'd already stayed. It was time to move the rifles to Williamsburg.

When Archer returned, Samuel was in the barn with a man Field had never seen before.

"Mr. Archer," Sam said as he approached, "may I present Sarah's son, Isaac. He came to collect his mother and bring us news of Lord Dunmore's actions in the county."

Field dismounted. Isaac stood as tall as he and appeared to be about Amity's age, but his eyes were like his mother's. He didn't miss much.

"I was just tellin' Sam that Lord Dunmore's commenced raidin' on the county. We heard soldiers were in the Dismal Swamp looking for powder."

"Did they find it?"

"Not yet. They spiked nineteen cannon."

"Papa! Papa!" A little girl with brown curly hair and the same startling blue eyes as Isaac's rushed into the barn with Delany in her wake. "Look what Miss Delany got for Susan. It's purple. My favorite color." Isaac bent and picked up the little girl.

"Gentlemen, if you will excuse me." Isaac turned and walked away with the little girl talking about purple but stopped to thank Delany.

Delany's face broke into a bright smile that Field had not seen in years. A stab of irritation ran down his back.

"You did it again." Sam smiled at Delany.

A hint of color rose in her cheeks. "I'm famished." She turned to head back out of the barn. "I'll go to the kitchen to see what Betsy has lying around that I can eat."

Field's stomach growled. "I think I'll go with you." He fell in beside her.

Sam stayed back without a word.

"I have not seen you alone since we arrived."

"There really hasn't been an opportunity, Mr.

Archer." Delany smiled as she looked up at him. "I slept late this morning."

"You deserved it." He offered his arm.

The same teasing look from last night crossed her face, but she took his arm. This time without rigidity, her hand rested easily on his forearm.

"I owe you," he said.

"You owe me nothing."

"Quite the contrary. You saved my life, and I was less than gracious about it."

"I suppose it's hard for a man to be rescued by a woman."

"It's hard for a man to be rescued."

That same teasing look challenged him again.

"Must you always quibble?" he replied.

"No. In truth, I don't know why I always find something to quibble about with you." She said this with her head down as though she had given it much thought.

"I will concede. It is hard for a man to be rescued by a woman."

They arrived at the kitchen. Field had not often been in a kitchen since he was a boy. At home, the food was requested and brought to him. He never had need to visit the cook. His mother took care of organizing his meals, and abroad, he'd eaten in taverns.

The square brick building radiated heat. Laughter escaped through the tall open windows. He'd assumed the inside was similar to the kitchen at Archer Hall. The large main room was painted white, and in the center was a long board table. The far wall housed the large stone fireplace that fed the family. Betsy stood in the middle of the room mixing something in a large earthenware bowl. Behind her were other servants occupied in various stages of food preparation. At the table was the source of their laughter.

Wiley, or Freewill, as he was apparently now known, was sitting at the table with a plate of biscuits and a cup of coffee.

"Wiley," Delany shared that brilliant smile again, "how are you feeling today?"

Freewill responded with a wide grin. "Better, Miss Delany. It's sore, but Betsy says I'm gonna be all right."

"Betsy." Delany turned to the small woman. "I'm starving."

"Sit down, Miss Delany." She turned to him. "Is you hungry, too, Mr. Field?"

"Yes, ma'am."

She smiled. "You don't have to ma'am me, Mr. Field. I'll feed you. Now sit down."

Freewill laughed, and Betsy laughed with him. Like his parents, their discourse was playful but underpinned with love and understanding. They were both on the same side. They saw the world the same way.

Field took a seat across from Delany at the table.

Betsy placed ham and biscuits and steaming cups of coffee in front of them.

"Freewill," Delany started, "tell me why you chose a new name."

"Well, Miss Delany, it's like this. We got us a new preacher. He's been preaching for the last month or so.

He tells lots of things from the Bible." Freewill stopped to take a bite of biscuit. He washed it down with coffee. "One day he told about our freewill. Anyone who wants to come to Jesus can do just that, he said. It's our 'freewill choice,' he said. Well, I knew it then, Miss Delany." He paused to look around the table. "After I was freed, I took your name. Wiley Button. That was me. Now I have the names of the two who freed me: Freewill Button. That's my name and always will be."

Field cleared his throat. It was a nice gesture for Delany to free a slave, but how was he to care for himself and a family? It was obvious he had no education to speak of. How could they expect to survive? "How do you provide for yourself and Betsy?"

"The Good Lord gonna take care of us, Mr. Field." Betsy's sharp response slapped him into her reality.

They wanted a chance. Like anyone else, given the opportunity they would succeed, or they would fail. At least now, they had the choice.

"Now, Betsy," Freewill soothed. "I work a piece of land that Miss Delany gave me, and Betsy and I work for Mr. Samuel."

Field nodded his response.

"It's a sweet thing to work for yourself, Mr. Field. A sweet thing."

"I have often thought so during my time in London." He smiled at Freewill and was given a smile in return. "I worked alongside my father's factor. There were many days I wished I was back home on my farm."

Isaac stepped into the kitchen.

"Delany, the doctor is here. My mother thought you should know."

Once again, Delany radiated charm in response to Isaac Harrison. He didn't know why that should bother him, but it did.

Delany turned back to face him. "Mr. Archer, would you care to walk back to the house with me? There is something of which we should speak."

Field's pride surged. "It would be an honor."

Outside, she took his offered arm once more. "The doctor told Mary that she has to stay put until the baby comes. He thinks it may be soon."

"Does that mean you need to stay, too?"

"Normally, no." She looked up into his eyes, the silver softened to gray concern. "She asked me to stay with her, and I told her I would."

"I can proceed without you."

"Not without my credentials, you can't."

"I am concerned for your family. Lord Dunmore sent Philips after me. That puts all of you in danger."

"If Lord Dunmore sent Philips after you, he wouldn't have let you go on the bridge."

"What makes you so certain?"

"Philips would kill his mother if it meant he'd make a ha'penny. He saw an opportunity and took it. That's all."

"I'll need to speak to Samuel before I decide."

She nodded her accent. "I'll go see the doctor."

12

Field found Samuel Fleet in the back of his barn.

"Archer, I was just on my way to see you and Delany." Samuel, now older, was a bit shorter, thick of limb and trunk. His presence spoke strength. Strength of body, strength of character. And he wasn't pleased about something.

"What about?"

"The boxes left on the wagon."

"Precisely the reason I came to find you."

Field told his story of bringing the guns to Williamsburg, Delany's insistence on helping him, and her need to get Ben home.

"I need to get the rifles to Williamsburg as quickly as possible."

"I'm afraid Delany is right. You will need her to move around in the counties."

"My concern is for your family. If it's true that Josiah Philips is after me for Lord Dunmore then my presence here puts you all in danger."

Samuel frowned and raked his fingers through his beard. "Josiah Philips is an opportunist. He preys on the weak. He looks for the unprotected and picks them off. He takes cattle, chickens, anything that might be of use to himself."

"So you think he wasn't after me in particular."

"I'd say not. He's cunning. If he'd wanted you, he wouldn't have let you go at the bridge." Samuel swiped at the dust on his pants. "I think he grabbed you because he could."

"Has he bothered you out here? Stolen your cattle?"

"Nope. It's an odd thing about free men." He raked his fingers through his beard once again. "They're loyal. They fight for their land. We all work together here. We protect what is theirs and what is mine."

"I take it you have freed your slaves."

Samuel's eyes narrowed, body tensed. "What're you asking me?"

"It's illegal. How did you manage it?"

"I didn't 'free' them. They bought their freedom."

Of course. "How did they afford it?" Field ran a hand through his own hair and asked, "When it comes to that, how did you manage it? Your holdings are large."

"Not as large as they once were. We never had as many slaves as the big plantations. At most, we had ten. When they decided to purchase themselves, I only had eight."

"Do you regret it?" he asked.

"No. My burden is lighter."

Isaac Harrison strode into the barn leaving Field wishing he could probe Samuel more on the matter. Delany Fleet's lofty ideas were one thing. Living in her house in the city, she was in the same category with that preacher, Wesley. Nice idea, but hardly practical. What did a shopkeeper or a city cleric know about mass producing tobacco or hemp or anything else?

His father's plantation was large, and the labor to run it was equally large. Hundreds, at least. He'd no idea how many slaves his father owned. Freeing hundreds of people without a plan was sheer recklessness. They'd starve with no land to employ them and no houses to shelter them. He couldn't very well turn them out on a whim. If he did turn them out at all.

My burden is lighter.

"Isaac. We'll break the hemp in two days' time. Are you available?" Samuel asked.

"I can manage it."

"Archer?"

"At your service." Until then, he would have to get to Kemp's Landing and check with the militia.

~*~

The rope of Mary's bed creaked as Delany approached the room.

"Then I can help you," a hopeful Mary addressed Ruben.

"Mrs. Tabb, you are free to do as you wish. My recommendation is to stay here in this bed until the baby comes," Dr. Woodsmartin interjected and closed his bag. He stopped short of treading on Delany's feet as he approached the door. "Mrs. Fleet," he puffed in exasperation, "I have instructed Mrs. Tabb in the best course of action. What she chooses to do is on her own head. Should you or the other Mrs. Fleet desire my services again, you have only to send for me."

Ruben sat on the bed beside Mary and took her hand.

"Dr. Woodsmartin, we are so very glad that you came to look after our Mary." She stepped into the hallway in front of him. "We would very much appreciate your attendance tomorrow," she whispered.

"Very well." He nodded and trod off down the hallway.

Delany re-entered the room to find Mary attempting to pull herself up to a sitting position. For the second time since she arrived, Delany could feel the love and concern between two of her friends. This time it was the strain of Ruben's heart as he navigated the tricky situation his wife laid before him.

"It's time to break the hemp," Ruben finished.

"Then I shall help you."

Ruben hung his head.

"I need to be about, Ruben," Mary pleaded. "I can't just lay here all day when there is work to be done." Mary looked to Delany when she entered. "Miss Delany, you tell him. I'm not used to all this laying about. I need to do something."

Delany took a deep breath. "We talked about this. We have to wait on God's timing. Little Ruben can't be born in the tobacco field on your way home."

"I feel much better now than I did this morning. I feel like a new woman." She swung her feet onto the floor.

Ruben did not let go of her hand. "Mary." His voice was soft. Delany almost didn't catch it. She felt she should look away but couldn't. Mary stopped moving. "Mary," he said again. "Please."

Mary glowed then. Her entire body responded to the call of his heart. She slid her feet back under the covers, never taking her gaze from the face of her husband. "All right, then," she said, "but bring me something to sew. I can't lay here doing nothing."

Delany slipped from the room. She needed quiet to process what she had just seen. She sat on her bed in front of the window. The reds and yellows of the maple were reminiscent of the straw-colored hemp that would be worked in the next days. The process of her life and marriage had been no different from the processing of hemp.

Her father had loved her, but Tom had not. In fairness, she did not love Tom. They came together because it suited Tom. Even Samuel and Molly had not shown her the raw scene she had just witnessed between Ruben and Mary. How had she missed the powerful thing that went on between two people who truly loved each other?

Longing swirled with the sadness that grew in her heart. She would never experience what Mary and Ruben had. The only man she ever loved thought of her as nothing but a servant. She paced the room.

But she loved Ben, and Ben loved her. She didn't know her other nieces and nephews as well, but there was no doubt that she would love them just as she loved Ben. How could she not? She loved Lucy, and

Lucy loved her. The brown depth of sadness began to lighten. Perhaps that was the answer. After they delivered their cargo to Williamsburg, Field Archer would be gone forever. Rather than remove to Northumberland where she knew not a soul, she could settle here and love and be loved by her nieces and nephews.

Perhaps Sarah was right. Maybe Isaac needed a wife. She didn't love Isaac any more than she had loved Tom. But he was good man, and she did love Lucy. She would just have to wait and see on that score, but the first part of her plan was sound. She would sell the estate in Northumberland and move to be with her family. The smoky longing that had constricted her heart relieved its squeeze, and she felt as if she could go out and face the others once again.

13

Dinner at the Fleet farm was always a boisterous occasion. Tonight was no different. The family, interspersed with their guests, ate their fill of roasted pork, sides of turnips floating in butter, cabbage, and corn fritters.

Field seemed to be in his element as he joined in the clamor without reservation. A small sad string tugged at Delany's heart. He must miss his home. His family was even larger and plenty rowdy around the dinner table as she recalled.

"So what do you say, Delany? Shall we have goose or turkey for Christmas this year?" Sam's eyes sparkled with amusement. She knew he didn't care. He found his joy in his Savior and his family. She glanced across at Molly, who mirrored Sam's merriment.

"Goose. I like traditional things."

"Times change, Miss Delany," Isaac teased.

"Times do change, Mr. Harrison, but we help keep our values by preserving some traditions."

"Food. Food will help keep our values?" Isaac laughed.

Delany felt the color rise in her cheeks. "Feasting. That preserves the values. I just like goose for

Christmas."

Isaac smiled back at her, his countenance warm and inviting. "Good save."

She nodded her response and looked down the table for a safe place to rest her eyes. Field had crossed brows. She didn't know what upset him, but she was glad it couldn't have anything to do with her. She was all the way at the other end of the table.

In the parlor after dinner, the younger children formed a ring around Lucy Harrison and Susan to admire the lavender riding habit Susan wore to dinner. Annette, nine, and Mary Ann, seven, their own Archer creations in hand, clearly coveted the latest in doll fashion. David, the eldest at fifteen, sat opposite his brother, Ben, at a game of chess. Margaret, eleven, chose a spot near her mother with her needle and cloth. Three-year-old Christopher presented himself to Delany with outstretched arms.

"Up."

Delany lifted him into her lap and gave him a squeeze. Her heart swelled with tenderness. Yes, there was much to be said for being an aunt who was loved.

"Aunt Delany, did you bring us a present, too?" Mary Ann asked.

Annette grabbed her arm. "Mary Ann, you don't ask things like that."

Delany smiled at them both. "Of course I did. Come with me."

Six pairs of wide eyes focused on her. "All of us?"

She laughed. "Just the girls. I'll bring back the boys' presents."

"May I come, too?" Lucy piped in.

Delany looked to Isaac, who nodded his assent with a wide grin. "Of course you can." It was so close to Christmas Delany brought extra presents, and she was glad she did. The tension of the last weeks in Norfolk were finally loosening. It felt like a holiday.

The wonder in the eyes of the children and the laughter that erupted at odd times added to the joy as her body relaxed. She could even keep Field Archer in perspective here on her own turf. Why this felt like her turf instead of her own house was still a mystery.

The girls bounded into the room behind her and climbed up on the bed.

Delany dug down into her trunk and produced three more cloth wrappers. She had labeled them by ribbon color: blue for Margaret, red for Annette, and yellow for Mary Ann.

Two wooden boxes of map dissections, one of England and Wales, the other of Scotland, were for the older boys. A third held a coach and six for Christopher.

~*~

For Field, the room cooled when Delany left it.

"She never forgets the children." Molly smiled at Sarah and turned toward Field. "I am certain that every girl child within her reach has one of your mother's dolls. They are treasured around here, I can tell you."

"My mother will be gratified to hear it."

"When did she start making dolls?"

"I believe she started when she was but a girl. My father told us that she tore many a pocket keeping her carving knife secreted for use at any time."

Molly and Sarah laughed.

"I bet she became a master of the darning stitch." Sarah focused back on the sock she was stitching.

Field laughed. "I wouldn't know about that. I can vouch for her ability to mend anything."

The ladies smiled with a nod and returned to their work. Silence embraced the room.

This whole room was like his family on a typical after dinner gathering. His mother would sit in her chair working. Sometimes it was a doll or a Nativity. Sometimes it was mending. His father would read or play his violin. Their children, his brothers and sisters, were seldom quiet. Of course, the youngest in this house were upstairs with Delany. When they returned with their restless noise, the home would more closely resemble his own.

Field's contentment deepened as he sat next to the fire. It was as close to the feeling he had at home as he had gotten in the last four years. Four years. He would never do that again. It was too long to be gone from hearth and family. They had written, of course, but he still felt detached from them. As the eldest of seventeen, some of his youngest siblings had barely been in short pants when he'd left. He hoped he'd recognize them and that they would recognize him.

The closest to him was Amity. Still unmarried, Amity lived at home. Her letters had been filled with dances and parties but no suitors. It puzzled him. At twenty-seven, she should have been married and have at least one or two children by now. Perhaps she, too, was holding out for love. It had never occurred to him before that their parents' example of love and affection in marriage could be a hindrance to their children's happiness.

He had been fifteen when he'd charged into his father's library and caught his mother on his father's lap in a secluded window seat. His mother had tried to hop out of his father's lap and compromising position, but his father's arms held her there.

"What can we do for you, Field?" His mother actually giggled.

He had forgotten what he came for and turned to escape. Neither of them called to stop him. He was still waiting for the woman who would love him like that, who would conspire with him and giggle.

If he'd been willing to settle for someone with the proper credentials and skills, he'd have been married years ago. Even Horsey Hester would fit that bill. Was Amity holding out, too?

The girls ran into the room before Delany, clamoring for their mother's attention. Each was showing their new doll dresses and, with the exception of the eldest, asking for help to change the dress of the dolls. Lucy Harrison climbed up in her grandmother's lap and rested her head. As the girls arrived, Christopher ran out the door.

Delany came in carrying three boxes in one hand with Christopher on her hip.

Field stood, but Isaac beat him to her side.

"Let me," Isaac said relieving her of the boxes.

"Thank you." Delany bent down to place Christopher on the floor and sat on a low stool next to him.

Isaac handed the boxes to her with a smile that she returned, much too gladly for Field's liking.

Delany gave Christopher his box and helped him open it. The child's eyes filled with glee. It was a fine set of coach and six. It recalled his own sets of coaches and soldiers and the happy hours he'd played with them.

The map dissections made by Spilbury were some of the finest he'd seen. The mahogany wood still smelled of the polish used to bring it to a shine. The maps were the very latest. What fine choices Delany had made for the boys as well as the girls.

Later, Field lay in bed staring out at the night. In two days' time, he would work like a field hand breaking hemp. It had been years since he'd beaten the straw until it revealed its inner fibers. He took a deep breath. It would be good to stretch his muscles. He'd been inside too long.

Delany's bright smile brushed across his memory. She was relaxing, and no wonder. Norfolk, with its threat of fire and quartering troops, would strain anybody's nerves. On her family's protected ground, Delany blossomed. All through dinner, she'd laughed and teased as he'd not seen her do since she was a child at Archer Hall. The children delighted in her and she in them. Except for him, she'd engaged with all of those present including Isaac Harrison.

Harrison would be a good match for her. He was close in age to Delany. She clearly liked him and doted on his daughter. They were well-suited in station also. Unlike himself, Isaac Harrison was a farmer, not a plantation owner. Delany would fit right in to Harrison's world.

Field's own world was different. He had a plantation to run. There was the General Assembly— when the current crisis was over anyway. He had every expectation that he would succeed his father in civic duty as well as familial duties as head of the Archer household.

Isaac Harrison didn't have the same responsibilities; he didn't need to travel in the same circles—places that a former servant would never fit in. All of this was logical. It was fact. It rankled.

Was he starting to care for her? Surely not. She'd caught his eye, and that was all.

He had not seen her equal in all his search for a wife. He had not been able to stop thinking of her since they had become reacquainted two weeks ago. He was almost prepared to forget the unsuitability of her former indentured servitude. On the issue of servants, he had not yet run into her like. Not only did her servants eat at her table, she was friends with former slaves. Her former slaves. At least one of them. It would never do.

14

"You shouldn't go alone." Samuel leaned against a sturdy bookshelf in his library while raking his fingers through his chestnut beard. "I've been so busy, I haven't been out to the house in a couple of weeks."

"Really, Samuel. You know I can take care of myself." Delany reached out her hand. "You have only to give me the key."

Samuel's fingers toyed with his beard, the hefty key in his other hand. "I'm too busy to escort you today," he spoke as if she hadn't said a word. "I'll speak to Archer."

Delany stepped forward and reached out her hand farther. "That won't be necessary."

"I'll speak to him anyway," He handed Delany the key as he passed by her to exit the room.

Delany hurried up the stairs to retrieve her cloak, but before she could make it across the yard to the lane which led to Tom's house, Field was at her heels, firelock in tow.

"I was told you might need some company."

She threw him her most withering look. Hopefully, he would just go away. She didn't want any memories of him in Tom's house. She would fill it with the laughter of her nieces and nephews, not with tears over what might have been. It would be hard enough to say good-bye to him this last time. Despite all she'd done to guard herself, she still liked his company more than she cared to admit. She didn't want to spend the rest of her widowhood bumping into his memory in her own house.

"As I told Samuel, I can take care of myself."

"Mrs. Fleet, I have no desire to overstep your wishes, but it isn't safe."

"Safe for whom, Mr. Archer?"

"Well, me, of course."

She had to laugh. They continued to walk toward the lane.

"Well, then, you should stay here where there are plenty of people about to protect you."

"Ahh, yes. Except, you see, this time, I am the one with the gun." He grinned.

She felt her face burn. She'd been in such a hurry to outrun Samuel and Field that she'd forgotten to bring her rifle.

"I will concede that I forgot my gun," she said with a nod.

The road that led to Tom's house was lined with trees in full fall glory.

"It is a lovely day for a stroll. Might I ask where we are going?"

"Tom's house." Delany pointed toward the bend in the road, "You can't see it for the trees, but it's just there past the curve in the road."

"I didn't realize there was another house."

"Oh, yes. Tom's father built two houses: one for each of his sons. He'd hoped to keep them close to home."

"It didn't work."

"No. Tom couldn't stand to be away from the city for more than a day or two. So Samuel has kept it for me. They use it for a guest house when theirs is full."

"So, not that often."

"Right."

Field stopped.

"What is it?"

"Sssh." Field placed a finger across his lips. He looked in front and behind them. "I can't see another soul on the road."

Delany smiled. It was true. There was no one, only the two of them. Just as when she'd followed him around as a girl. The sun-caught edges of his brown hair glowed red. His face relaxed into a look of appreciation. Only this time she wasn't a girl, and the house they were about to visit was her own.

"If I have my way, I will never go back to London," Field stated and continued down the road.

"Never seems like a long time for a planter such as yourself. I would think you would enjoy the society and the activities a large city like London has to offer."

He paused in front of her. They were close enough that she could reach her fingers into the red glow and test its smoothness.

"There is not one street in London, unless maybe in the deepest hours of the night, where one may walk and be alone. Certainly none so peaceful as this." His amber-brown eyes shone with joy at his surroundings.

Father God, give me the strength I need for when he goes home. I don't know how I will face it again. "You have missed your home, I think," she said.

He stopped, brown eyes taking in her features. "More than I can tell." His soft voice caressed her ear and sent gentle waves down to her heart. He was close enough to kiss her, dangerously close.

Dangerous.

She swung away from him and continued toward the bend in the road.

The house came into view once they had passed the curve in the road. Set back from the road, it looked like an etching with a brick façade and symmetrical windows on either side of the front entrance. Long grass bent in the breeze. Samuel had taken good care of Tom's house.

Delany pushed the key into the lock. The tumblers fell, and she pushed the door open. Field followed her into the spacious hall. It was as she remembered. Honeyed wood lined the walls below the wainscoting; burgundy wallpaper rose to the ceiling. It appeared to be in good shape. Not so well looked after as if it was lived in, but it hadn't gone to seed either.

Empty. It was peaceful and quiet and empty. There was no ghost of Tom lingering in its shadows. Delany took a deep breath and let it out slowly. Peace entered her heart as it soared with thanksgiving. She could make it her own.

She followed the hall past the staircase, through the large room at the back of the house to the back door. On the back porch, as she had instructed, stood her waterfall. The only interest she'd ever shown in the property was to add the waterfall. She hadn't been back since Tom's death, fearing something she couldn't name. Now she knew her fear had been without foundation.

"You are very quiet." Field was close enough that she could smell the scent of leaves he carried with him. She turned to face him.

"I'm trying to decide what it was I expected when I came here."

He looked puzzled. "Have you never been here before?"

"Oh, yes. Yes, I have, but not since Tom's death."

"Did you love him very much?" He looked down into her upturned face.

She moved away to lean against the porch railing so she could breathe and think at the same time. "No. I didn't love him. He loved me. Or at least he said he did." She looked down to hide her eyes.

"What were you expecting?"

"Not sure. Ghosts, maybe. We never lived here together. Never spent even one night." She looked out over the outbuildings: the kitchen, the laundry, the smokehouse—all stood unoccupied. She would need to inspect each of them. She looked back at Field. "But it was Tom's house, and his father consulted with him on major aspects of the project. I guess I expected to feel his presence in the imprint of his tastes, but I don't." She looked up at him again. "It's as if visiting my father's grave. He's not there. For me, it's a fruitless pastime."

"I see you made at least one contribution." He pointed to the waterfall.

She laughed. "Yes. Once I discovered the waterfall, I knew I would want one wherever I lived, so I ordered three and had one installed here."

"Where is the last one going?"

"Button Cove."

"What's that?"

"It's my estate in Northumberland County."

She stepped down on to the brick walkway that led through the dependencies. She didn't find any major damage. Field stayed by her side in true bodyguard fashion. Inside the main house she found nothing that a good cleaning wouldn't fix to impede her removing and taking up residence.

Delany found Field in the library, adjacent to the dining room, staring at the almost bare shelves.

He reached over and took the two volumes off the shelf. "I think I should return these to Samuel."

"What are you talking about? I'm sure they must be Tom's."

"I'm surprised to find them out in the open. They are of a subject matter that shouldn't be displayed. And certainly shouldn't be shown to a lady."

Delany felt her face color. She had run across other similar volumes when she had cleaned out Tom's effects from their home and even in his office at the shop. "It's not the first one I've found. Don't give them to Samuel. I'll dispose of them in the fire."

"Samuel must not have used the house in a really

long while if these were lying about." His query crinkled his eyebrows. "You don't think anyone else has been here, do you?"

"And left them sitting on a shelf like a bouquet of roses? I wouldn't think so." But she made a note to ask Samuel.

"I'll carry them for you," he offered when she reached for them. "You wouldn't want to get caught by one of the children with them on our return."

"Gracious, no." She put a hand to her chest and looked around the room. "Well, I think we're done here. Tomorrow I shall go to Kemp's Landing and hire some staff."

"That brings up another topic we need to discuss," he said as he followed her down the hallway toward the front door. "I need to meet up with the local militia. Perhaps they can get the goods to Williamsburg."

"Or at least get a message to Williamsburg about the goods," she responded.

"Exactly."

~*~

The village of Kemp's Landing consisted of Main Street, a small avenue near the crossroads of Princess Anne Road and Witchduck Road at the end of the eastern branch of the Elizabeth River. Large, wooden tobacco houses surrounded the waterfront. George Morgan's store stood in the center of Main Street across the mud-crusted road from Billy White's Tavern and Livery. At the far end stood the blacksmith's shop, smoke billowing out of its chimney.

The seemingly haphazard arrangement of the buildings lent a friendly feel to the scene. Folks called out greetings to each other as they bustled about which added to the warmth of the place. Vastly different from the gruffness of Norfolk, which teamed with merchants and sailors.

Delany sat next to him in the wagon in an indigo riding habit that drew attention to the redness of her auburn hair and the cool gray of her eyes. As the wagon swayed, she would dip near enough that he could smell clover and a hint of dandelion. She had worn her hair up in its usual twist, but he wished to feel it net across his face again. *Stop. That kind of thinking will just get you into trouble.*

"I'll get out right here," Delany said. "I'll be in Morgan's."

He hopped down. When Delany stepped into his raised hands, a spark hummed through his body. She stood on the ground caught in his arms and looked into his eyes. *Did she feel it, too?*

She stepped back and spun on her heel. "I shall be in Morgan's should you finish before I do. If not, I could meet you at the blacksmiths or at White's." Her voice, a little shaky, steadied as she detailed her plan.

"White's. I'm already getting hungry."

She smiled and walked across the street into the store.

Field drove toward the blacksmith's shop. Sitting in a wagon at Kemp's Landing, the very last thing he expected to see was the long, loose-limbed gait of

Simon Morgan. Simon walked like a marionette, with steps that were sure in his own mind but were uncertain to those watching. And to dispel any disbelief Field might ascribe to the situation, Hester Morgan was right beside him.

Hester's features were unmistakable. The eyes were still just a touch too far apart and the hawk nose stood out, but age had been kind to her. Her chestnut hair shone in the sunlight; her skin, while not as fine as Delany's, was smooth. At fifteen she had been a horror; at twenty-five, while not a beauty, she was not unpleasing to behold. Hester walked with deportment and grace, but that could be said of any woman who walked on the arm of his ungainly friend.

Field dismounted. "Simon Morgan!" he called and clasped his friend in his embrace. "Whatever brings you to this little village?"

"So you've come home," Hester commented before her brother could respond.

"Field Archer. It does my eyes good to see you, man."

"We are staying with our cousins. We are on our way to White's for luncheon, and you are welcome to join us."

"I am not alone. My companion just went to Morgan's. I am on my way to the blacksmith on some business."

"Perhaps another time then," Simon, always generous, offered.

"Of course you should come out to the house," Hester agreed. "I am sure my aunt and uncle would be delighted to meet you."

"Where are you staying so we can send the direction?"

Surprised at his reluctance, Field responded, "I'm presently residing with the Fleets."

"The merchants?" Hester grimaced.

Field's irritation spiked. "Yes, they've been most kind and attentive since I've returned."

"Didn't Amity's little friend—I forget her name—marry one of those Fleets?"

"Yes, she did." Field tried to contain his annoyance, "But he died some time ago."

"How sad for her." Hester spoke the appropriate words without conveying the sentiment usually associated with them.

"Yes, I believe it was."

Mary's words came back to his mind. *Flat and hard like a shilling.*

No. I didn't love him. He loved me. Or at least he said he did.

Had it been sad for Delany when Tom died? She hadn't appeared sad or remorseful when he'd accompanied her to Tom's house. Still it was possible that she missed him. She'd said she didn't love the man, but that didn't mean they weren't friends.

"You should bring her when you come to visit." Simon always was too smart for Field's comfort. Simon's keen observations had made Field uncomfortable on more than one occasion. "The more the merrier I always say, and there are precious few young people like us about."

Hester shuttered her objections and replaced them with a false smile. "It truly would be lovely to see her again. We can speak of old times."

"If we arrange it properly, we could have enough people for a spot of dancing." Simon smiled wide. "I'd love a bit of dancing with pretty girls in the evening. And if I remember the right girl, Delany, was it? She was very pretty, indeed."

Field nodded his agreement. Intoxicating might be a better word, but Simon was right. He'd never seen a prettier woman than Delany Fleet. Introducing her to his friends, however, was not exactly what he'd had in mind. Of course, she already knew Simon and Hester. Simon would not care about her origins, but Hester did, and she wouldn't be the only one.

"I will convey your invitation." What more could he say?

He drove to the blacksmith shop wondering if Delany knew how to dance.

Sweat formed under his hatband as soon as he stepped into the shop, which comprised one large room with a partition counter to separate the back from the front. Arranged on tables in the front were various implements for sale. The back held the heart of the blacksmith's trade and the source of the oppressive heat. A large forge sent streams of smoke up the chimney. There were tables along the walls scattered with different tools waiting to be repaired. One table held dozens of firearms in various states of brokenness.

A man, with arms the size of small roof beams, stood sweating next to the fire.

"Mr. Parke?" Field called.

"Aye. What can I do for ye?" William Parke let his hammer hang to his side and moved to meet Field in the front of the shop. Parke wore a hat pushed down over blond hair. His forehead was broad; his eyes were blue and severely bruised.

"I've been told that I can find Lawson and Hutchins here."

The man separated his feet to shoulder length apart and brought the hammer head to rest in his other hand. "Who told you that?"

"Fleet said I should tell you that sunflowers grow among the barley."

Parke did not relax. "What do you want with them?"

"Passage."

"Passage to where?"

"Williamsburg."

"Why?"

"I'd rather talk to Hutchins and Lawson."

"I'll tell them ye called. But they'll not be able to help ye. No one can get past Lord Dunmore right now."

Suffocated, he swung away from the blacksmith and looked out a window into the street. He couldn't tell if it was the heat wafting from the forge or the situation he was in or a combination of both. What was he to do? He'd thought once he got out of Norfolk the rest would be easy.

"Where can I find Hutchins right now? He has to work and live somewhere."

"We've heard that Williamsburg has sent troops."

Field breathed deeply. "How did you hear that?"

"I'll not be tellin' ye everything I ever knew."

"Fair enough. Will you tell me who blackened your eyes?"

"Soldiers. Came in here yesterday and broke the guns."

Field took a closer look at the pile of guns. Some were spiked; and others bent and shattered.

"Can you repair them?"

Parke nodded. "Given the time."

15

Delany sat down at a table in White's and looked out the window. She would have to do something about her garments. All the women within her range of sight were dressed in homespun. Her blue brocade made her stick out like a peppermint in a basket of potatoes. She'd gotten more than a few nasty looks in Morgan's.

She'd known it was coming, of course. The boycott on British goods required economy. Just like liber-teas. If one was a patriot, one drank tea like a patriot. If one was a patriot, one had better dress like a patriot. At this point, she saw no reason to throw away perfectly good brocade in favor of homespun.

"Please forgive the intrusion." Delany looked up to find a tall, blond gentleman standing across the table. "I believe we have met. I am Simon Morgan. Might you be—"

Of course she remembered Simon Morgan. How could she forget the boy her friend had such feelings for? She smiled at him and stood to offer her hand. "Delany Button. Well, it's Fleet now."

"I thought that was you when you came in. I'm delighted to meet you again." He had a wide smile that went all the way to his heart with no guile. She liked him at once. "Might I reacquaint you with my sister, Hester?"

Out from behind him stepped a tall, chestnut-haired woman. Her hair was piled up higher than her brother's head. She was dressed in court-like finery of a deep green, woolen riding habit that perfectly set off her chocolate brown eyes—eyes that looked down her slope of a nose at Delany.

"Mrs. Fleet, I do believe we met before at Archer Hall on one of my many visits there. You were Amity's little friend, were you not?"

"Indeed, I was. It's kind of you to remember me." She turned toward Simon, "Is Morgan's your family store?"

"Certainly not," Hester replied quickly. "We are no relation to them whatsoever."

Simon looked a little befuddled at his sister's retort.

Before Delany could reply, Hester's face lit up at something over Delany's shoulder.

She turned to see Field smile and make his way toward them. He stood behind her, close enough that she could feel his warmth.

"Archer, we were just getting reacquainted with Mrs. Fleet. Just about ready to make our invitation before we head for home," Simon said.

"Mrs. Fleet," Hester interrupted, "my aunt and uncle are hosting a small gathering at their house on Saturday." She delivered another lofty smile. "We would be delighted if you could come."

"Thank you for the offer. I shall have to consult

my calendar and get back with you."

"We shall send along the invitation directly," Hester said clearly not believing that anything could possibly be in the way of her party.

Field nodded to them both as they left the table and made their way out of the tavern. He took the seat opposite her own.

"What a nice man. I haven't seen him in so long, I'd forgotten..." Delany started.

"Did you hear there was a raid here a couple of days ago?" Field's eyebrows knit together, and his look became fierce.

She leaned in closer. "Keep your voice down," she warned. There was no telling who was about out here. She knew some of the townspeople but not enough to make her comfortable. "I heard some talk in Morgan's"

"What can I get ye?" A young boy stood at Field's elbow.

"Some coffee, I think," Delany told the boy.

The boy looked at Field, and he nodded in return.

"What did you mean that you have to check your calendar? Do you have any other invitations for Saturday?"

"No. But I would like to think about whether or not I want to go and not be forced because I happened to see someone in a tavern who felt obliged to invite me."

"I'm sure Simon genuinely desires your company."

"And Hester?"

The coffee arrived, and Field looked down into his

cup. "Simon is my best friend in the entire world. I wouldn't offend him for anything."

Yes, but what does that have to do with me?

He caught her gaze when he looked back up from his coffee. Was it longing she saw there? Was he lonely, too? He shielded his feelings before she could gauge what it was but not before her heart responded to his vulnerability. She wanted to throw her arms around him and hold him.

"Shall we go then?" she asked.

His smile disarmed her. "I think we should."

"All right, then. I'll accept the invitation as soon as I receive word from them. If I receive word from them. I'm still not convinced that Miss Morgan was being anything more than polite. I also find I am discomfited at the prospect of a party with so much unrest about us."

"Life must continue. Farms must produce food so people can eat, and life must go on."

"I know you are right, but having a party at such a time seems...unseemly."

~*~

Field waited until they'd cleared the last building before he spoke again. "The blacksmith had at least fifty weapons that were destroyed in the raid."

"Where was the militia?"

"Mr. Parke was less than forthcoming with information. He says he will fix the guns, but it will take quite a bit of time."

"Seems like God put you in the right place at the right time."

"I was thinking the same thing." He was glad she had the same instinct. "But I didn't get a bead on Lawson or Hutchins."

"There's time."

He found peace in her declaration though there wasn't really time with the war heating up around them. There was no question: it would be war. But he'd seen God in action around him before. The militia here clearly needed his goods. He would give his weapons to this cause. When he had the opportunity of doing so, he would leave. His safety would be in God's hands.

They hit a rut in the mud-caked road, and Delany bounced into him leaving a trace of clover and dandelions.

"I almost forgot. The blacksmith said they'd heard that Williamsburg has sent troops."

She looked up at him and smiled with warmth in her silvery eyes. "Thank God."

He was looking forward to Saturday night very much.

~*~

Two days later, Delany said good-bye to Sarah. Tears blurred the carriage into a brown cabbage as Delany waved to Sarah, Lucy, and Isaac. Pungo was less than a day's journey away, but when the tears welled up, Delany couldn't stop them.

"Why do things have to change so?" Molly put her

arm around Delany and led her to the house. "I was content with my shop. My house."

"Let's have some tea."

"All this change makes me weary. It's too sudden and violent. I feel as though I have no control over my life." Once seated in the dining room, Delany crossed her arms on the table and put her head down. Her emotions swung from right to left.

Sarah was gone to the bosom of her family where she belonged.

Where do I belong?

When the tea arrived, she took a deep breath, sat up straight with dry eyes, and took the plunge. "I'm thinking of removing to Tom's house."

Molly's mouth dropped open. "Do you mean permanently?" She placed her hands, palms down, on the polished surface. "Besides, it's no longer Tom's House—it's your house."

"Well, yes, I know that, but we've never called it that before."

"Don't be silly. It's your house."

She couldn't tell Molly about her newfound feelings of home that she'd experienced since she arrived. Molly had always done her best to make her welcome. That Delany never felt that way was no fault of Molly's.

"What about the shop?"

"I'll keep it open as long as Mr. Harris is willing to keep eyes on it for me. After that, I'll have to see."

"If this blows over quickly, perhaps you can stay. If not open, at least retain your property."

"I hope so."

"You'll be closer to Sarah and Isaac out here." Molly's eyes twinkled with knowing.

"Sarah, yes. Isaac?"

"It's been a long time since I've seen two men fight over a woman. The last time was, hmmm. Let me think." She put a finger to her lip. "It was me." She grinned, a brazen look in her eye.

Delany cringed like a school girl.

"I've noticed Isaac has been more attentive than usual, but I assumed it was on Lucy's account. I've noticed no other attention."

"If that Field Archer scowled at Isaac Harrison any harder, it would be an official challenge."

It was Delany's turn for a gaping mouth.

"You're mistaken. Field Archer is not interested in servants. And former servants are just the same as servants." Despite Delany's attempt to keep her voice even, the look in Molly's eyes told her she'd failed to keep her feelings hidden.

"So it's Archer."

The flush rose to Delany's cheeks. It was over. She poured herself another cup of tea and told Molly the story she had never told a soul. Not Sarah, not even Amity when she'd gone the next morning to return the pink silk gown.

Amity had been so thrilled with her evening, especially the dances with Simon Morgan, that she'd barely noticed Delany's absence, first attributing it to dancing and the sheer numbers of people at the party. When she'd realized that Delany was actually gone from the party, it was very late, and Amity had assumed she'd gone to bed.

Delany had never corrected her friend's error. Now, she told Molly the whole tale all the way to John Crawley's awful pronouncement.

"He did not say such a thing."

"He did."

"Rotten man."

Warmed by the camaraderie, Delany smiled. "So you see, you must be mistaken. I know he misses his family. Perhaps that is what you see." As much as Delany wanted to believe that somehow Field had changed, that he could see in her as a woman to be loved, he wasn't capable of that.

Molly reached across the table and took Delany's hands in her own.

"Maybe you should take a second look at Isaac. He's a good man, Delany."

"Yes, he is," Delany conceded, "but I'm not looking for a husband." She took a deep breath. "I thought I would move to Northumberland. But that dream has died. I think I will stay here in Tom's—my—house."

"We'll be so glad to have you here."

16

The moon was huge when Field handed Delany up into the waiting carriage. Loose leaves rustled in the breeze. Wood fires scented the air with the promise of winter.

Samuel and Molly had also received an invitation and were traveling in the carriage in front of them.

"It was nice of your friend to include me in your invitation. I'm still puzzled by it."

"Simon Morgan is a generous man. He remembered you and thought you would make the numbers for dancing. You do like dancing, don't you?"

"Are you worried I cannot dance?"

"Of course not." He cleared his throat like a guilty man covering his tracks. "I merely wondered if you enjoyed the activity."

She laughed at the irony of his worry. If he'd stepped out with her all those years ago, he would know the answer to his question. Dancing was a refined activity. Her father had made sure she could dance so she should be a proper gentleman farmer's daughter.

"I can dance. I love to dance."

He turned toward her, and her heart swelled at the

sight of him silhouetted in the moonlight. "Perhaps you would do me the honor of standing up with me this evening."

Delany smoothed the skirt of the indigo silk skirt she'd chosen for tonight, remembering the borrowed pink gown and glad that even in this proximity, he could not hear the pounding of her heart. "If there is dancing, and it has not been promised that there will be, then I will, indeed, stand up with you," she answered. Against her better judgment, Delany glowed at the thought of dancing with him. "Will it be a large party?" She thought it best to keep up the conversation rather than let her heart fill her head with dreams that would never come true.

It's just a dance.

Breathe.

"Simon didn't say, but I was given to understand that there is not an abundance of younger people about for a proper frolic."

"I'm afraid that is true."

Silence fell between them. Delany and her racing heart could think of nothing else to say. She trained her gaze on Samuel and Molly in the carriage in front of them.

"I saw little Ruben today. He's quite a boy." Field said. "Have you ever assisted in a birth before?"

"No. It was my first one." Little Ruben's face, his tiny dark eyes glistening in the morning sun, floated across her memory. Her face flamed at the memory of a dream of a plump little boy with brown hair that glowed red in the sun and amber-brown eyes.

"Did you and Tom ever have a child?" He clearly didn't know how to proceed.

"No." She wasn't sure why she answered the outrageous question except that little Ruben's face played across her memory. And the truth that she had no children and never would have children was too real to her in the moment to dissemble.

"Were you frightened?"

"I was prepared to be frightened," she replied and laughed a little. "I thought I would be when Mary first asked me to stay with her. I think Molly thought I would be scared. When I got there to her room everything was very tactile." She turned to look at him.

He had inclined toward her while listening intently.

"I'm a practical woman. When I arrived, there was work to be done. I did it, and really, that was all. Except this one thing." She took a deep breath and added, "I am now sorry that I will not have children of my own."

The sounds of creaking wood, springs, and wheels stretched between them.

Delany itched for the ride to be over. She'd said too much. What would he think? "How do you feel about escorting a former servant to your friend's house for a frolic?" She'd done it again, perhaps because he'd had nothing to say about the most profound revelation about herself she'd had lately.

Field cleared his throat and slowed the carriage.

"Don't have an answer?" she goaded.

"Rather, it's I'm forming an answer." The vehicle

came to a stop. He turned toward her, features illuminated in the uncolored light of the large moon. "This is what's between us. All this time."

"Yes." Her heart pounded. Hands fisted in her lap. She wasn't supposed to care what he thought anymore, yet she did. She found she still cared a great deal. But this would be the last time she'd risk her heart for him. Just this one time she wanted—no, needed—to know. Then it would be put to rest for the remainder of her life. She would know what he thought of her.

"You are not a servant."

"Certainly not. But I was once, and I have it on the best authority that you would not dance with a servant."

"What an idea. Of course not. I would not have an occasion to do so." He reached for her hand and held it in both of his own. "I find you to be a most remarkable woman."

Her mind stopped cold in its tracks.

"I am honored to escort you this evening and any other evenings, when it comes to that."

It was as though the Lord shut her mouth. She could say and do nothing but allow him to hold her hand. His warmth faded from it as he picked up the reins and continued to the Morgans'.

~*~

It was the first thing that he'd felt right about since he'd set his feet back in Virginia. Delany was remarkable. He would know. He'd met enough females in the last four years to last a lifetime. It'd never occurred to him that her prior servant status would bother her. Always confident. Always in charge. Her vulnerability called to his protective nature. No one had better offend her tonight, least of all him.

Morgan Hall was lit up to glory.

Delany took Field's offered arm and entered a hallway of tall, molded ceilings behind Samuel and Molly.

Heated perfumes laced the air. Music competed with voices offering greetings. The hall was as he remembered it, closed and dark and then opening into a large ballroom at the back of the house.

"Archer, glad you came." Simon grabbed Field's hand.

"I believe you remember Mrs. Fleet," Field said.

"Delighted to see you again, Mrs. Fleet. You remember my sister, Miss Morgan."

Hester stepped up to her brother's side. She wore burgundy woven with silver gilt. Her hair was pulled back from her face and while not tall enough to catch fire on the chandeliers it was the tallest rig he'd seen since he'd been back in the colony.

"There you are, Delany Button. Oh, it's Fleet now, isn't it?" She smirked.

Delany nodded her assent.

"Outside of our recent meeting at Billy White's, I don't believe I've seen you since that Easter Party at Archer Hall when you ran away so abruptly. I do hope this evening you will find reason to stay."

Run away from a party at the hall? Out of the

corner of his eye, he saw Molly stop at Hester's words.

Before Field could respond, Delany answered for herself. "I'm sure I will, Miss Morgan. You were very kind to invite me."

"You'll get used to me, Mrs. Fleet." She smiled broadly, looking down from her five foot eight to Delany's even five feet, "I am plain spoken. Come. Let's find some punch." Hester and Delany moved away together with Molly in their wake.

Plain spoken was one way to put it; rude was another. Delany could take care of herself, so he'd let it go this once.

Field moved toward Simon's aunt and uncle who were ensconced in matching wingback chairs on opposite sides of the fire. A vision of Jack Sprat and his wife in reverse, Mr. Morgan filled his chair with length and breadth, and his tiny wife occupied naught but the corner of hers.

"So, Archer, what do you think? Shall we have a new nation or remain faithful to a tyrannical sovereign?"

"Mr. Morgan," scolded his wife, "give the man a chance to get his punch before you badger him."

"I don't badger, Mrs. Morgan. I just wish to know where he stands."

"It seems we are set in motion whatever it is that I think," Field responded.

"There may be some truth in that. It will be safer for those who stand with the patriots than against."

"As you say, sir. It's well that my inclination agrees with their choice."

"Well said, sir." Mr. Morgan, wig slightly canted to one side, face glistening in the heat of the fire, took a long draft from his tankard. "Go and get you some punch, my boy, and welcome."

Field found a place to stand next to Simon and the punch bowl. The room continued to swell with a steady stream of arriving guests. Each time a new guest appeared, the room would turn with one face and send a welcome greeting. Not aloud, but one of good feeling and generosity. As new people made their way around the room, they experienced the warmth of the welcome. Field extended his felicity to join the others until the newcomer was Isaac Harrison. His wellspring dried up, and his humor soured.

"Your sister is looking well tonight," Field said to Simon as he watched Harrison make his way through the well-wishers toward the punch bowl.

"Indeed. It took her most of the afternoon to prepare. I can't imagine why she went to the trouble. You know what she thinks of provincial farmers."

"Perhaps she's set her cap?"

"If so, you'd better be careful. I've not seen her dressed like that since we've been here. And you and Harrison are the only new faces."

"Perhaps Harrison?"

"Definitely not."

"Thanks for the tip."

Field collided with Isaac at the refreshment table. "Harrison."

"Archer."

"Didn't know you'd be here," Field said.

"The Morgans are old family friends," Isaac grimaced. "I suspect they are in cahoots with my mother to find me a bride."

"And do they succeed?" Field asked.

"Like you, when the time is right, I will choose my own wife." Isaac drank from his glass. "If you will excuse me, I see the Fleets are here."

~*~

"So, the competition continues," Molly indicated with a slight tilt of her head toward the approaching Isaac Harrison.

Delany's good-sense fight against an enraptured heart consumed her thoughts, blinding her to the events at her elbow. At Molly's prodding, she took notice of Isaac Harrison dressed in a dark green coat and buff breeches exactly suited to make his remarkable eyes glow. Over his shoulder, she observed Field with Simon Morgan.

Field's gaze locked with hers, and she felt her face turn pink. She turned at once to Isaac.

"Delany, I am pleased to find you here."

Delany's stomach tightened as she remembered Molly's comments about the two men. She would have to pay closer attention this evening. "Did Sarah come with you?"

"No. She's with Lucy." In her peripheral vision, she could still see Field.

His brows knit together as though he'd smelled something rotten. At the first pluck of the fiddler's tuning string, Field stepped toward Delany.

Isaac offered his hand.

To refuse him would have been rude. She tilted her head in assent and laid her hand in his. She kept her gaze rigidly before her so as not to glance back at Field and embarrass her partner.

The Morgans were successful in their numbers. Everyone who wanted a partner had one. Only older couples remained on the sidelines chatting. Field was paired with Hester Morgan. Except for the superior look on her face, they did make a fine-looking couple. He was a bit better looking than she, but she made up for it in grace if not exactly in her manners.

Hester did look extremely becoming in her burgundy brocade with silver petticoat. Candlelight caught on the silver thread woven through her burgundy mantua. Her hair was done in the latest London fashion with lace and silver flowers threaded throughout. Strategically placed hair pieces made the whole confection stand magnificently high.

Delany could never endure that much frippery. It was just too impractical for her. How in the world would she be able to bend over and pick up a wee tea set for a customer if her hair bobs were in danger of falling out? But she had to give recognition where it was due. Hester's look was stunning and far outdid anyone in the room.

The dance started, and she focused her attention on Isaac. He danced beautifully, meeting her at every turn with a smile in his blue eyes. When they were together, he inquired after Mary and the baby. A woman could do worse than Isaac Harrison.

After four dances and four partners, none of them Field Archer, Delany moved toward the punch bowl. The lemonade was cool and refreshing, but the open window even more so. She placed herself in front of the breeze and opened her fan. Perhaps she would sit the next one out.

"Mrs. Fleet," Field bowed, offering his hand. "Would you do me the honor?"

Girlish flutters shook her hands. Hopefully, he would attribute it to the coolness wafting in through the window.

He led her to the dance line. Across from her, he stood in midnight blue. The amber of his eyes twinkled mischief. He looked like the young man she'd fallen in love with more in this moment than he had the entire three weeks they had been together. Had it been only three weeks?

I am still in love with him.

The revelation caused a quiet calm to enter her soul. Awareness became her primary sense. The light in Field's eyes told her he was enjoying himself. She smiled at him. His eyes softened, and his face opened into a smile. Did he feel it, too?

They glided together into the movement of the dance, her hand minute in his. Her spirit nodded to his even as her head inclined toward him in the maneuver of the dance. She was his and always would be. She could not stop the inclination of her soul to blend with his anymore than she could willfully change the color of her hair or the shape of her feet.

It would be a lonely life, but she had tonight and the next few days. Once they delivered the rifles to the militia, he would be gone. The look in his eyes as he softened toward her would forever be imprinted on her heart.

She passed under the arch of his arm, a whiff of fallen leaves and soap filled her nose. She looked up and was caught by the awareness in the honey flecked amber of his eyes. A gentle wave of hope rose in her heart that she could not quell. If he felt the same, might they have a chance?

They crossed places with Isaac and Hester and came to rest in their next position. Hester's face was cold and aloof. Isaac's eyes pierced her in return. Awareness had its drawbacks; one could easily be distracted. She turned her attention back to Field only to find him in a scowl as well. All traces of the dear look in his eyes were gone.

As the last notes of the song resonated through the room, her heart grew restless. Chatty voices invaded her awareness.

Field escorted her back to the open window. He poured them each some lemonade.

"Mrs. Fleet, how do you like living in a busy port town?" Simon asked as he reached for a glass.

"I like it most of the time. Right now, I am considering removing here."

"Indeed?"

"Yes. It seems we are destined for war. There are threats from every quarter of burning the city."

A small group that included Molly and Samuel

joined them.

Delany and Field stepped back to make room.

"Delany, Molly and I just discovered that we both attended the Braxton School for Girls in Williamsburg." Hester gushed like a thirteen-year-old girl. Delany was repulsed.

Molly gave her the same look she gave her daughters when they were overly exuberant.

"Of course, I was a few years ahead of Hester. We didn't know each other at school," Molly said.

Hester colored at the remark. "Well, of course I never said we knew each other there, but isn't it a lovely coincidence that we could have?"

Molly had come from a well-to-do family in Williamsburg, but Delany had no idea that she had attended the prestigious Braxton school.

"I think Braxton is the epitome of what a school should be. What is your opinion on girls' schools, Delany?"

Field stiffened behind her.

"I'm sure you are right that Braxton is an excellent institution," Delany answered. "But I have wondered why a girl's education is deemed to be inferior to a boy's. I mean, why not have both sexes attend the same school and receive the same education? Female minds are not inferior to male minds after all. We're just trained differently."

Hester's face went as red as her gown; her blue eyes narrowed. "I myself received an excellent education, and I am looking forward to running a household for my husband when the time comes." Her gaze left Delany's for a flash, presumably to cast a glance at Field, who stood behind her.

Really?

"I am sure you will," Delany said, wondering why she was the object of Hester's ambush. "If you will excuse me." She exited the group and headed for the door and a cool breath of fresh air. *Is this what living in the country would be like?* She stepped out onto the porch and wished she'd thought to bring her cloak. At least it was quiet. Perhaps she should rethink her decision to remove from Norfolk.

"May I join you?" Field came outside.

She stepped back and leaned against the railing. In the light of the window, his angular features appeared primal. Hair escaped its curlew, jaw cut from granite, evening growth shadowing his cheekbones. His nearness called to her heart, but the reality of their situation had been made very plain by Hester, whether it was her intention or not. Delany did not fit in his world, and she never would. The dreams her heart had woven as they'd danced were just hot air dissipated by the cold reality of her recent confrontation.

A gracious woman like Molly tolerated her because she was family by marriage. It was not an association she would have sought out.

"I'm not fit company at the moment."

"Fit for whom?"

"The likes of you."

He took a step closer and leaned on the railing next to her. "By the likes of me? Do you refer to me as a gentleman?"

"Norfolk is made up of business men and women. People who came to Virginia for a chance to make a new life for themselves, to choose their own destiny." She turned and looked out at the fields surrounding the house. "They were willing to pay any price for their destiny. My father was willing to do anything so that he could own his own land. He dreamed of being a gentleman farmer." She snorted. "Pretty funny, huh?"

He turned to face her. "No. Your father was an admirable man. I've heard my father say so many times."

Delany sought his gaze barely visible in the light of the window. "I don't have the same education as Hester or Molly, but I own a successful business in the busiest port in the colony."

"Some would argue that Alexandria is busier."

She could just see the outline of his devastating grin.

"They're wrong." She grinned back.

"People say stupid things wherever you go, Delany."

At the sound of her name on his lips, her breath caught. She longed to take a step closer. "I suppose you're right. But I think I must take another look at my decision to remove here."

Field took a step closer and reached for her hand.

Her heart rapped a steady beat.

"I think we have time for one more dance before we leave, if you would care to?"

Later, they rode back to the farm in silence behind

Samuel and Molly. Images from the night played across her memory out of sequence in a blur of confusion. In a shaft of moonlight, she saw Molly rest her head on Samuel's shoulder. It was the most intimate gesture she'd ever seen between them. She shifted another inch away from Field. She would never know that pleasure. She wrapped herself deeper into her cloak and remembered the softness in his eyes and gentleness of that smile.

18

"The only woman I saw anyone fighting over was Hester Morgan," Delany told Molly the next morning after breakfast when they were alone in the parlor.

"You're too close to see what's going on," Molly said as she glanced up from her mending. "The only one I saw fighting was Hester. I think she's got her eye on Mr. Archer."

Delany let out a frustrated sigh.

"Imagine trying to lay claim to me by the Braxton school." Molly chuckled as she made the next stitch in little Christopher's shirt. "I hated school."

"You did?" Delany couldn't keep the astonishment out of her voice.

"Oh, goodness, I tried to get out of it every day."

"You? Always correct Molly?"

"I know. Don't tell my children," she giggled.

"Do you mean that my lack of school doesn't bother you?"

"Of course not. God has a plan for each of us. Yours didn't include the Braxton school, and if I were you, I'd thank Him for it every day." She laughed again.

Of course He had a plan; she just wished she could

figure out what it was. Should she stay or should she go back to Norfolk? When Delany looked up from her thoughts, she found Molly gazing at her.

"You should ask Him. He has the answer."

"I tried that. I just don't seem to be hearing it. I don't know if it's because He's not talking or because I'm so jumbled up inside that I can't hear Him."

"I know what you mean. Perhaps the path He has for you is not one you are currently considering."

Yes, well that may be, but what am I to do in the meanwhile? I'm in love with a man I can't have. Like it or not, it doesn't matter where I live. I'll be miserable anyway.

~*~

Three days after the dance at Morgans', Field's heart still lurched every time he thought of the smile Delany gave him before their first dance, which was just about every waking minute. He would have to be more careful. He'd nearly kissed her on the porch. And while Hester was completely wrong in what she said and did, her opinions were common among his social circle. He didn't care if Delany had been a servant or not. She was smart, brave, and intoxicatingly beautiful. Like Isaac Harrison, he would choose whom to marry, and he wasn't interested in anyone's opinion on the matter. But could he subject Delany to that for the rest of her life?

This trip was taking much longer than Field had anticipated. First, he thought he'd be home for the tobacco harvest. Now he'd be blessed if he got home before Christmas. The longer it took the more complicated his leaving became. For that matter, the more complicated his staying became, too. He was beginning to suspect that his attraction for Delany Fleet was becoming something more than a passing fancy. He needed to leave before something happened that he could not undo.

Soon he would deliver the guns to the militia, and once he'd done that, he would leave. He owed it to Samuel to help him repair the damage done by last month's hurricane. They had a few days more work to do. If the rain held off, they should be done by week's end. Then he could go back to Kemp's Landing. This time he would go alone, and he would find Lawson.

He was glad Delany had decided to relocate closer to her family. It would make him easier to know she would not be alone when he left. Before he went, he would confirm that there was nothing amiss at Tom's house.

"When was the last time anyone occupied Tom's house, Sam?" Field asked as they rode in the wagon. Today they were going to mend Freewill's broken fence.

"Delany asked me that same question a couple of days ago." He cast a sideways glance at Field. "Last Christmas. Molly's folks and a bunch of her cousins came to stay, so we put them up out at Tom's house."

That didn't sound much like a group that would keep the kind of books that he'd found in the library.

"Did she tell you about the books we found?"

"No, she didn't."

"Well, that's not surprising. They were not the kind of thing a lady would discuss—or should even know about."

"Did Delany see them?"

"Not as such, no. I noticed them and carried them back here. They are in my room. I haven't burned them yet because I wanted to talk to you first."

"What would I have to do with them?"

"Nothing specifically. Delany said she ran across more like that when she was cleaning out Tom's things after his death."

"That doesn't surprise me." He took another look at Field. He was quiet for a minute and raked his fingers through his beard. "My brother ran with a pretty wild set. They all disappeared after his death, except John Crawley. I heard he helped Delany out quite a bit when Tom first died. I don't like to speak ill of anybody, but those fellows were not the kind of people I would like to have around my wife and children."

"Well, that doesn't help with the origins of the books."

"No."

"Whatever happened to the other slave Delany released?"

"George?"

"If that is his name."

"I've a hunch he's still around here somewhere. He's supposed to marry Pauline, but I haven't heard anything more about that in a long time. I also haven't seen Pauline crying about it, so I don't know."

"Could he be at Tom's house?"

"Don't think so. I check on the place every week or so, and I've never seen him there. Besides, he's a bad sort."

"I don't think she should go there alone."

"She should be all right. Even if he is there, George has no reason to harm Delany. She freed him. He should feel indebted, if anything." His eyes twinkled with merriment, "Besides which, I'm sure you've noticed that Delany is a fully grown woman with a mind of her own. If she wants to do something, she'll do it, and there's nothing you can do about it."

Her brother-in-law's lack of concern troubled Field. Didn't he see how fragile she was? He could still feel the imprint of her tiny hand in his while they'd danced. He could crush the bones in her finely made fingers should he wish it.

The flash of Delany's silver eyes challenging him came to mind. He would have to come up with some reason to accompany her on her visits to Tom's house. The more time went by, the more he was convinced that someone was hiding there.

Freewill and Ruben were working on the fence section by a dirt road no wider than a wagon. Sam steered the wagon alongside the boundary. The broken lines ran at least a mile.

~*~

Delany and Molly joined Betsy in the kitchen. Betsy had prepared food for the men repairing the fences, and Molly thought they should bring the children and make a picnic.

The sun shared the sky with rolling cloud drifts. Delany's spirits were buoyed by the fresh air. She spent so much time inside her store or her house or here, she'd nearly forgotten how peaceful it was just to be out in a field where one could see God's creation in all directions.

The children jostled themselves around in the back of the wagon bouncing more than once into Betsy and the food hampers.

Delany saw Field first, dressed in a pair of Sam's brown work breeches and a white shirt open at the throat. Even from a distance, she could see the strength in his biceps and the rest of his lean, hard body as he lifted a large fence rail into place. He wiped his face with a handkerchief and waved as the wagon approached.

"I hope you brought water," Sam said as he approached Molly to lift her down from the wagon.

Field came to Delany's side and raised his arms. Delany stepped into his embrace. He lifted her down with ease and stood with his hands on her waist. She put her hands together to keep them from reaching into his tousled hair. The warmth in his amber eyes and glad smile made her heart skitter.

"Of course there's water."

Molly's statement brought her back to the present. She sidestepped away from him, and he moved slowly out of her way as though he'd been swept away too.

Field and Delany spread out quilts for everyone

and soon sat down to ham and bread and Betsy's specially made bread-and-butter pickles. Betsy had just sliced the large cake when Delany heard the familiar sound of canteens clinking and the rustling of soldiers marching. Her innards clenched cold. She looked around for the children.

They clustered around Sam and Molly.

"Go to the wagons," Sam said quietly.

Delany stood and picked up the plates.

Field picked up the quilt.

They'd put the first load in the wagon when the sounds stopped.

"You there," the soldier in front hollered. "Who's in charge here?"

Sam took a step forward still close enough to hold Molly's hand. "This is my land."

Molly kept the children around her waist except for Ben and his older brother David.

The two boys stood just behind their father's shoulder.

"By order of His Majesty's Royal Governor, Lord Dunmore, we seek provisions for His Majesty's men."

Delany blanched. This was a raid. They would take anything they found. *Dear God, please keep them out of the barn.* There were about ten uniformed men and one dressed in the clothes of a gentleman. He stood just behind and to the left of the leader. *Why was Josiah Philips here?* Field moved closer and took her hand. The warmth of his strong body soothed her jitters. Longing to slip under the protection of his arm, she took a deep breath and stood straight. Any display of affection could put them in danger. One just didn't know where one stood when the soldiers came, and Josiah Philips was not an indicator of good things to come.

"We've just finished our repast. You are welcome to the remainder—"

The man laughed with a voice scraped with gravel. "We aim to come to your farm."

Sam and Molly and their children rode in one wagon.

Betsy and Freewill stayed behind to go to their farm.

Field drove Delany in the wagon they had used to bring the food.

Once in the wagon, Field pulled her close to his side. This time she didn't move away. His nearness gave her comfort. He wouldn't allow them to hurt her.

"I've never seen a civilian traveling with the Regulars before," Delany whispered to Field keeping her eyes on the wagon in front of them. *Molly must be sick with worry.*

"My thoughts exactly."

"What do we do?"

"We follow Sam's lead. I suspect they're just here for food. Didn't you say they've been raiding along the river front?"

"Yes." Anger flared. "What about the barn?"

"They have no reason to go to the barn. There's no food there. They brought their own wagon."

Delany was comforted by his confidence. Short lived comfort, soon her mind was racing over the possibilities of discovery. "Let's pray," Delany offered.

Field tucked her under his arm. She prayed for the Lord's protection for each of them, especially the children, and the safety of their cargo.

The soldiers scurried around them like ants kicked out of an ant hill.

Sam and Field placed the wagons in front of the barn and dismounted.

"Go to the house," Sam told Molly.

Molly huddled her brood around her and headed toward the house.

"Stay with Molly and the children," Field commanded as he dismounted.

Delany reached for her rifle with her foot. Brandishing it would likely get it destroyed. She grasped it in her right hand letting it settle in the folds of her full skirt. "I'm staying here."

Field's contours hardened. Suddenly weary, Delany stiffened with rage, ready for his argument. It didn't matter what he said, she would do the right thing. Who did they think they were coming down here to take their food? What if something happened to any of them? No, she was staying right here to do what she could to defend them.

Field grabbed her hand and pulled her into the shade of the barn. "Delany," he lifted her face to capture her gaze, "please". It was so quiet she wasn't sure she heard it. "Please," he said it again.

Anger deflated. Was the concern she saw in the depth of his brown eyes just for her? Delany turned toward the house.

The soldiers raided the smokehouse first.

Delany was halfway to the door when she heard him.

"We meet again, Mrs. Fleet."

"Go on," she said to Molly. Her rifle hung heavy at her side. Delany turned to face Josiah Philips on horseback.

"You are too beautiful a woman to be in homespun. You were made for finer things, Mrs. Fleet." The glint in his eyes was unmistakable and more threatening than anything she'd ever seen in John Crawley. He would enjoy hurting her.

"What are you doing here, Josiah Philips? Can't the soldiers find their own food?"

"Sure, they can, but I told them about your farm out here and what abundance you do have. And they just had to see for themselves. Since they didn't know where you lived, well, I agreed to show them." He grinned at her. Evil rolled off him in waves.

The first one hit her stomach like nausea. Her spirit engaged, and she stood up stronger.

"Get lost, Philips."

Field's arrival at her side was unexpected and very welcome. Solid and strong. He took a step to stand in front of her.

"Until we meet again, Mrs. Fleet," Philips said with a nod of his head. "And we will meet again. I assure you I will see to that."

The waves hit her again, but this time she felt them roll off and away as though she was covered by a shield.

Field took her hand. "Get in the house and stay

there. I will come when they are gone."

Delany ran to the house.

Molly was waiting on the other side of the thick, windowless door. "Who was that?" Her face was pale. Wisps of angel-blonde hair were plastered to her scalp. She rocked Christopher in her arms. "He made me sick." Mary Ann and Annette held onto her arms. Ben paced with hands behind his back. David had gone with his father and Field.

"Me, too." Delany shook out her hands and upper body. "Let's not allow him to overset us. They will be gone soon."

Molly's eyes darted back and forth. "I don't like him. I want him to leave. Here. Right. Now." Panic fueled the staccato in her tone.

Delany reached out for Molly's hand. Molly grasped onto Delany and held hard. "They just want food, Molly. They won't harm us today."

The darting gaze came to rest on Delany's face.

"I've seen this happen hundreds of times in Norfolk. It's just Captain Squire. He's stealing food. He won't touch us today," she said soothingly. "I promise."

Everyone's gazes searched her face with the same intensity. "Come to the window." She pointed to the soldiers walking in and out of the smokehouse. "Look over there. They took a ham. See them put it in their wagon?"

The soldiers threw beef and pork into the wagon and headed toward the chickens. A soldier came out of the storehouse with a half barrel of flour.

"If they take all the food, what are we gonna eat, Mama?"

Molly's eyes cleared at the fear in Annette's voice. She reached out and pulled her into her embrace. "The Lord will provide. He always does." She ran her fingers through the little girl's hair and held her close. "He always does." Molly looked at all of them. "Let's all go to the back parlor. We have better things to do than stand here and worry about what we can do nothing about." She shooed them down the hall taking one last glance as the soldiers headed toward the wagons in front of the barn.

19

It had taken every ounce of strength he had not to shoot Josiah Philips on sight. Delany's tiny form standing defiant in front of evil perched on a horse was too much for his equilibrium. Every time the image played across his mind, he felt the need to clasp her to him and shoot the scoundrel.

After they left, Field spent his days and his energy mending fences and anything else Sam or Ruben or Freewill had for him to do. Keeping busy was the thing until he could get the guns to Kemp's Landing and get home. Today he was chopping wood—anything to keep him busy and out of Delany's path.

Dunmore's raids were more frequent. He was confiscating guns and ammunition every day. They didn't dare venture too far from the farm for fear of the soldiers' return. Dunmore or no, he would have to go soon.

"We're hosting the preacher on Sunday," Sam said walking up to the growing pile of wood.

"Who is it?"

"Craig Reid. I think you will like him."

And that was the other thing. He'd always been happy with his church. Now he found himself ensconced in a family of dissenters. More kind and generous people he'd never met. They knew more about the scriptures than he'd ever considered knowing, but if he had to hear another verse quoted at him, he'd hit something else. He steadied a half log on his splitting round, stood back, and swung the ax. The wood split with a satisfying crack. "I will look forward to it." He placed another half log on the splitting round.

"It won't work, you know."

Field leaned on the ax. "What won't?"

"You can't pound your feelings for Delany out on this wood pile." Sam spared a finger from raking his beard to point at the rounds waiting for his ax.

"I don't have any feelings to pound."

Sam chuckled. "I told myself the very same thing." He shuffled away.

~*~

It was a week before Delany had an opportunity to get back out to Tom's house. Perhaps she should call it Button Cove since she was no longer moving to Northumberland. It was a good sight better than thinking of it as "Tom's house". Yet it didn't feel like her house. It would take time and living in it to do that.

After breakfast, Delany and Pauline set out in a wagon loaded with cleaning supplies, a food basket, and her rifle. The morning was crisp with a breeze blowing that was just on the cusp of too cold to have the windows open. Dressed in a brown calico gown and petticoat that she used for cleaning the store, she was eager to get started on her future.

The past week had anchored her more to her plans of removing from Norfolk and remaining in Princess Anne. Mary and Ruben had moved into their own home. It was a blessing she would be able to live close to them. Watching little Ruben grow would be a delight.

Field had been more than distant. He was absent. Gone with the dawn, he appeared only at supper. He was obviously avoiding her to let what had passed between them at the Morgans' disappear. He'd nearly kissed her on the porch. Ashamed at how easily she had fallen into the old longing to be in his arms, she could almost be glad he was keeping so busy. Except she wasn't. The night at the Morgans' dance had flamed her interest but not satisfied it. One unguarded night to acknowledge how she felt had not sated the longing at the sound of his voice or the sight of his mischievous grin. *Stop. There's too much work to do.* Delany drove her thoughts to Tom's house just as it came into view. It was much bigger now that she faced it in work clothes. She hardly knew where to start.

Evie Seldon, and her husband, Thomas, would arrive at the end of the week. Evie was a cook and her husband a master gardener and groundskeeper. Sam had recommended the couple to her, and she was thankful they were available. Delany would rely on Evie and Sam to help her find the rest of the help the large house would need. Until then, she had herself and Pauline. Delany was no stranger to housework. In fact, she had an odd desire to complete quite a bit of the work herself. She planned to go through every room deciding what to keep and what to give away. When she was done, the house would no longer be Tom's house. It would transform into her own Button Cove.

Delany sent Pauline to clean the kitchen. She would start upstairs in the bedrooms and work her way down. She left the large front door open to let in light and fresh air. Then she opened every window and door on the first floor before heading up to clean. She did the same upstairs before focusing her attention on the main bedroom, the one that would be hers.

The room was half the size of the second floor containing the bedroom and a small nursery. A large four-poster bed stood three quarters of the way down the long rectangular wall. Thankful she'd never shared the bed with Tom, she had no scruples about keeping it. She reached up to take down the red floral bed curtains that Tom had allowed her pick, his only indulgence in furnishing the house. These she would keep. She folded them into a neat pile. Once she'd removed all the linens and folded them, she carried them downstairs and put them in the wagon.

A tall shadow passed the window of the kitchen. Delany picked up the rifle she'd foolishly left in the wagon. Standing on the stoop of the kitchen, she peered into the dark room. Blinded from the bright sky, she couldn't see much.

"Did you need something, Miss Delany?" Pauline, broom in hand, asked from the hearth of the large stone fireplace. A pail of water stood on the large trestle table in the middle of the room.

"I thought I saw someone in the window." Delany looked around the room.

Pauline didn't look frightened.

Delany walked past Pauline into the back room. Empty. "Did you see anyone?"

"No, ma'am." She went back to sweeping, "Just me here."

Something didn't feel right, but Pauline was there the whole time. No one could have gotten past her unnoticed. The tall shadow must have been just that. A shadow.

"I guess I better get back to work." No one knew she was here but her family. Even if the soldiers came, she had nothing to give them. Josiah Philips was a different story, but there was no reason for him to know of her whereabouts, least of all here at Tom's house. She glanced out the upstairs window. The yard was quiet. No strangers in all the acres she could see. Enough. She would not be a ninny.

She pulled down the linens in the other rooms making one-armed trips up and down the stairs to put them in the wagon so she could keep her weapon with her at all times.

By noon she had wiped down the wardrobe, dressers, and every other surface including the wainscoting in her room. *Her room.* She went to the windows and looked out over the fields that led to the Fleet farm. This would be her view. She couldn't see the Bay from her window, but she could feel and taste its salty breeze.

Even at this distance, she recognized him. He rode hard, his lean body tense with exertion.

Was everything all right? Had the soldiers come back? Had something happened to Mary or the baby? She rushed downstairs as he arrived at the front drive.

He alit quickly and nearly pushed her down in his rush through the door.

"Is everything all right?" she blurted, holding onto his forearms to steady herself.

"Are you all right?" he asked holding onto her waist.

"I'm fine." She straightened, but he did not release his hold on her waist. "I am cleaning my house."

"I came in for the noon meal and heard you were over here by yourself." The concern in his amber eyes dissipated her worry.

"You rode so fast I thought something was wrong." She put a hand up to her throat. "You scared me to death."

He dropped his hands from her waist and ran one through his disheveled hair. "You scared me to death. You shouldn't be out here on your own. It isn't safe."

Irritation crept up her back as he stalked up and down the ballroom. What was he so upset about? She would not have deliberately caused him trouble. She was used to taking care of herself. If he was so concerned, where had he been all week? "I appreciate your concern, but I am not alone. Pauline is here."

At once he towered over her.

She clasped her hands to keep them from reaching

up into his loosened hair.

"Not good enough. You should have Sam or Ruben or me."

"Mr. Archer, I can take care of myself."

"Can you?" He lowered his head and captured her lips. She stilled. His hands engulfed her waist. A gentle tug on her bottom lip and her decisiveness vanished. The years of waiting for him disappeared. She was fifteen, and it was her first real kiss. She melted into him, threaded her fingers through his hair, and poured all the longing and love she felt into their embrace.

A gasp startled them both.

Field pulled away, his chest heaving as though he had bounded up a flight of stairs.

Delany's heart pounded as though she had raced him up those same stairs.

Pauline stared at them from the doorway. "Sorry, Miss," Pauline fled the room.

"I'm sorry, Delany." Field scraped his hand over his face. "I shouldn't have done that."

Shame heated her face. Of course he was sorry. He would never dally with a servant. She turned from him. "Think nothing of it, Mr. Archer." She managed to say through her tight throat, "I'm a widow. You are not the first man to steal a kiss." *Just the only one to succeed.*

He reached out to take her hand.

She clasped them together in front of her waist. "Have you eaten your noon meal, or did you forgo that to rescue me?"

Dropping his hand to his side, he said, "I came

straightaway."

"You must be famished. There's a basket in the wagon and a cask of fresh lemonade." She started toward the door and the wagon.

"Delany." He caught her arm.

She swung around to face him. "Let's just put it behind us," she said, "as if it never happened." She hoped that he didn't see the tremor when she smiled.

"It did happen."

"I am aware of that, Mr. Archer."

"Aren't we past that now? Field, please."

She breathed deeply. "Field, I understand you are sorry and that it didn't mean anything. These things happen to widows sometimes."

His face stormed. "Stop talking."

She stopped short to survey him.

"That's better." He came to stand in front of her. Her senses came alive at his closeness. The woodsy sent of leaves, the tangy smell of the work he'd done all morning, and the warmth of his body called to her trembling heart. "I'm not sorry I kissed you."

Astonishment wiped away the trepidation. "You're not?"

"No. In fact if we stand this close for much longer, I'm liable to do it again."

Delany was glued to the spot, mesmerized by what he was saying and the softness of his lips as he formed the words. She placed her hands on his chest to confirm she wasn't dreaming. "I'm sorry that I was not more discreet. I didn't mean to be carried away like a schoolboy."

20

The crowd of people spilled out from the parlor into the main hall with some drifting into the dining room. Field had not seen this many people together since he'd come to Princess Anne.

Craig Reid moved easily among them with arms wide open and a creased Bible in his well-worked hands. Clean, cheap black suit. Black hair cropped close to the scalp. Blue eyes like a crisp fall day surrounded by fine lines that echoed mirth. Joy radiated from every movement. "Welcome, brothers and sisters!" he bellowed from his place in front of the mantel in the parlor. "God loves you, and so do I."

The warmth of his greeting rebounded in smiles and general greetings from the crowd.

"Open your Bibles to Revelation, Chapter 22, verse 17."

Field had never been to a service where he was told to open his Bible.

Pages started to flip in the room.

Delany's fingers fluttered through the Bible's pages, fluffed from use. She found the passage and angled it for him to see.

How like her to help him without thinking,

unobtrusively seeing what he needed and providing.

"Whosoever will may come." Craig's voice caught his attention. "We all fall short, brothers. But we are all welcome to come." The love radiating from this man could only come from God alone. Craig leapt from passage to passage weaving the story of salvation.

Field left the passage finding in Delany's capable hands while he continued to be fascinated by the words that came out of Craig's mouth. He must have heard these words before since he'd been in church all his life, but they took on a new meaning as Craig spoke them.

"God is no respecter of persons. If He loves me, He's got to love you the same. And brothers and sisters, He does."

The power of his words fanned out through the room and hit Field right in the heart. The experience was unlike any he'd ever had. His logical mind agreed with the text. But this time he could feel the pull of God's arms as He welcomed him into an embrace that Field knew would last a lifetime.

"Let's pray."

Field closed his eyes to pray but never heard the words. His heart overflowed with wonder.

"If anyone here would like to come and pray with me, now is the time."

Field's feet moved before his mind balked. Quietly, while the prayer went on, Field prayed with Craig a prayer that would secure his future for all eternity.

When he regained his seat, Delany reached for his

hand. Her silver eyes, liquid and soft, showed she understood.

"Welcome to the family." Sam gave him a handshake and back-slapping hug.

Field couldn't reconcile it all yet, but what had been presented to him was right. He took Delany by the hand and led her out to the large maple tree shading the back porch. "Do you know what happened in there?"

"Yes," she said with her arms crossed and her Bible next to her heart.

"There are times in your life when you have an epiphany, and it changes everything. It's not that you've never thought about the issue before or that you've been exposed to new information. I think it must be dependent on time and the space in which you receive it. All of a sudden, in a blink, something opens up, and you see it, whatever it is. And this time, I saw all eternity before me, and it was so simple. I didn't have to do anything but believe. He is real. Not someone I read about in a prayer book on Sunday. He is here now with us. Right now." He stopped talking, filled with the wonder of it all. His spirit expanded and filled his entire body. "How can this be?"

The breathtaking smile she'd bestowed on him the night they'd danced graced her face now.

People milling about kept him from pulling her into his arms.

"Momma's looking for you, Aunt Delany," Mary Ann said as she stepped between them.

"We will talk more later." She placed her hand on

his arm, and he covered it with his own.

~*~

The Indian-summer day heating up the shade could not deflate the exhilaration Delany felt after this morning's service.

Field would never be the same. He walked around with his Bible as Lucy carried Susan. He had asked her to write down the passages that Mr. Reid had used this morning, and she promised she would.

She would never forget the joy in his face when they'd stood under the tree together. As soon as the guests left, Delany prepared to go to her house. She wanted to hang the freshly washed bed linens and make a list of things to get for her next trip into Kemp's Landing. The time to herself would be a relief, for while she loved her nieces and nephews, she hadn't had two minutes alone. She was giddy and off kilter. Solitude to think about what was happening between Field and her was necessary. He had not told her that he loved her. He'd just kissed her ardently. Had he felt that kiss as she had?

She moved through her responsibilities and then got in the wagon heading to her house. It took an hour to replace the bed linens, including hanging the bed curtains. She stopped at the cherry writing desk in the corner of her room to write down the items she wished to pick up and order from Morgan's.

The view from her window was restful. She could see no one for miles. Sweat dripped from her face onto the foolscap, obscuring her words. The open window offered no respite from the humidity.

Surveying the landscape to confirm that she really was alone, she removed her dress and stays leaving only her shift. She grabbed a towel and a cake of soap and headed downstairs to the waterfall. She had filled it herself two days ago in preparation for a day just like today. Cleaning the large house was filthy work.

She would ask Freewill to enclose her shower as soon as he had a chance. Right now, it stood open on her back porch, a spindly set of pipes and a cistern. Peering outside the door to confirm once again that she was alone, she stepped out onto the porch. The cold water ran down her body in cleansing rivulets. She used the cake of soap to wash her hair. It was heaven to feel so clean. She wrapped herself with the towel and ran back up to her room.

Delany dressed using a clean shift from the trunk she'd already delivered. She left her hair down to let it dry.

21

They finally arrived in Kemp's Landing. People milled around, but Field detected a bit of desperation among them. A forced cheerfulness. Several flyers were posted for a ball to be held in two days' time at the assembly rooms.

"I didn't realize that Kemp's Landing had assembly rooms."

"We are provincial. We're not uncouth, Mr. Archer. We have dance associations and balls." Delany laughed at him. It was the first time she'd let down her guard since he'd kissed her in the ballroom at her house. Since then, she'd kept her distance or made sure they were never alone.

"I beg your pardon." He tapped the corner of his hat and bowed. A teasing smile played at the corner of his lips.

"You are forgiven. I think it might be just the thing to move our cargo."

Field agreed with her assessment. He just needed to find Lawson to do the hand off.

Delany disappeared into Morgan's with her list while he headed over to Parke's.

Parke nodded to him when he entered. "Archer."

"Mr. Archer, is it? A tall gentleman in a buff colored suit addressed him.

Field eyed him, not anxious to make himself known.

"I'm Lawson. I heard you wanted to see me."

Field looked to Parke for confirmation. Parke nodded. Field extended his hand. Lawson took it in a dry, calloused one.

They agreed that Lawson would receive Field's cargo at the ball two nights hence. Lawson would arrange men to transfer the boxes while Field danced with Delany inside.

The arrangement suited him just fine. This detour had taken enough of his time. He was ready to head home. He was anxious to give his mother his thanks for insisting he stop at Fleet's to bring her present. She couldn't have known what a difference it would make to his life—all of their lives—when he brought Delany Fleet home to be his wife.

Now he just needed to tell Delany.

Once they had cleared town and Field was certain they wouldn't be overheard, he told Delany of his agreement with Lawson.

"I find it nightmarish that a party will be had in the midst of these raids," Delany said.

"Life does go on."

"Yes, I know that, but it seems to me that when people are being killed and their farms are being raided that they wouldn't think of getting together to dance a jig."

"Perhaps it's just because all these things are going

on that they need to dance a jig to remember that better times are coming."

"I will concede that such amusements will continue, though I believe I will still be discomfited."

"Excellent. Then you won't mind if I claim a couple of dances with you?"

She hesitated, but her good manners won out. There was no way for her to decline without being rude, and he knew it.

~*~

Molly was in the parlor when they arrived home. Delany claimed the seat next to her sister-in-law. Molly made uniform stitches in another of Christopher's shirts.

"How does it go with Mr. Archer?"

"He will be leaving in a couple of days."

"Are you all right?"

"There is to be a ball in the assembly rooms in Kemp's Landing in two days' time. After that, he will leave for home."

"What will you do?"

"I will stay here and then remove to my house."

"What did you say you'd call it?"

"Button Cove."

The thought of living here with her family had sounded so full of life and purpose. But Field's kiss had uncovered an emptiness she'd been trying to forget. The vision of little Ruben's dark eyes seeing the world for the first time. The amber eyes of a plump baby boy with dark red-tipped hair that would never be born.

"Has he spoken to you?"

"No. He kissed me once. But no, he hasn't spoken to me."

"He has been attentive, staying by your side at Button Cove." Molly grinned at her reference.

Delany smiled in appreciation. "He has. But that doesn't mean anything, does it? He doesn't have much else to do and no servant to command to send in his place."

Something she wasn't seeing niggled at her conscience. It was something obvious she was sure, but she just couldn't place whatever it happened to be. Yes, Field had been attentive, but after that kiss, which he'd apologized for, there had been no declaration of love and no further kisses either. She was partly to blame for that. She took care not to be alone with him again. He was leaving and her heart would break as she stood there and watched him ride away. She would go to her house and live as full a life as God would give her, but her heart wouldn't survive if she indulged anymore in Field's nearness to her.

"Give it time, Delany. I think God is working on him. Archer doesn't know what he wants yet."

"Were you in love with Sam before he knew it?"

Molly put down her sewing to laugh. "Oh, yes. He fought it hard. He thought that being a farmer's wife wasn't enough for me, being the daughter of a planter."

"But you are happy."

"It took him some time to realize that I would be happy anywhere as long as I could be with him. But that was after he came to terms with the fact that he loved me. He thought he could do everything himself. Didn't need anybody but himself."

"Is it always this complicated?"

"Probably. But if it's worth having, it's worth the wrangle we go through to get it."

~*~

Delany woke early the next morning after a fitful night's sleep. She put on a muslin dress and prepared to go to Button Cove to clean the smokehouse, a square brick building with no windows and a dirt floor. She did not relish the task. She had been right to work on the house herself though. She had been exposed to every square inch of the building and its dependencies, with the exception of the kitchen, which she'd left in Pauline's capable hands.

Pauline would accompany her today as well.

After that, the ball would occupy her time, and then Field Archer would go home.

22

Delany dressed in her finest slate-blue silk mantua, with its lavender petticoat. The entire ensemble embroidered with silver gilt thread sparkled as she moved. It flattered her complexion and accented her silver eyes. Tonight would be the last time she would dance with Field, and she wanted it to be memorable for him as well as for her. It was the first time she'd ever regretted not employing a lady's maid. A maid could have made her curls frame her face in the latest fashion. As it was, she did her usual configuration of a bun at the back of her head but allowed a few tendrils to curl at her temples. It had a pleasing effect in the glass. She couldn't compete with Hester Morgan's finery, but then, she didn't need to. She was off the marriage market. Hester was still shopping.

Field awaited her in the hall with Molly and Sam. Field's blue suit so closely matched her own that people might assume there might be a purpose in it. She briefly wondered if she should change but thought better of it. Let them think what they thought. Tonight would be the last night she would have in his arms, and she would make the best of it.

Once again, they followed Sam and Molly in their

wagon. Field hung close to Sam believing there was safety in numbers.

Delany placed her hand over her pocket where she kept her travel documents just in case they should be stopped.

Lawson was outside when they arrived talking to the men who were directing the parking traffic. They were motioned to park next to a wagon Delany assumed was Lawson's. They were nearly through. When they came out tonight, it would be finished. Delany trembled as she stepped into Field's waiting arms.

The assembly room was a large wooden rectangular building ablaze with candles. Fiddle music spilled out the windows. The night was cool and smelled of tobacco and salt.

She took Field's offered arm and followed Sam and Molly into the party.

A country dance was in full swing. Bright colors whirled in and out of the movements of the dance. Those who chose not to dance sat or stood chatting on the sides of the room.

Field led her immediately to Simon Morgan standing next to the refreshment table.

Delany faced back toward the dancers, hoping to see Sarah. To her delight, Sarah stood across the room next to Isaac, who was talking to Dr. Woodsmartin. She excused herself from Field and Simon. Delany skirted across the line of dancers to present herself to her old friend. Before she could speak, Isaac intercepted her. The smile froze on Delany's face as she spied John

Crawley in the far corner conversing with another gentleman she did not know. *What's he doing here?*

"Is something wrong, Delany?" Isaac reached for her hand.

"Oh, it's nothing. I was just surprised, that's all." While she did her best to regain her composure, the dread she felt at the sight of the odious man cooled her insides.

Sarah's light touch replaced Isaac's. "Come. Let's get you something to drink. You look awfully pale."

They walked arm in arm toward the refreshments. When they arrived back at the table, Delany took a spot next to Field, who turned his body slightly to acknowledge her presence. She resisted the urge to tuck under his arm where she would be safe.

"What's John Crawley doing here?" she whispered to Sarah.

"I don't know, but I expect he's following the governor around."

"The governor is in the harbor in Norfolk."

"He's staying with the Logans at Kemp's Landing."

"Thank God that's all it is." She sighed a deep breath and took another look at Sarah. She was dressed in a mantua of Caribbean blue which made her normally serene eyes dazzle. "I don't think I've ever seen you out of your black."

"I'm tired of black."

Delany grinned. "It's time I came for a visit."

The music stopped, and the dancers departed the center of the floor.

Field's hand was in front of her before Isaac could take a step toward her. He nodded his head as she passed with Field for the dance floor.

"Has anything upset you, my dear?" he asked as he took her hand for the first movement.

Her head snapped up at the endearment. "Not really."

"You looked deathly pale when you returned from the other side of the room. If your friends hadn't been there, I would have taken you outside."

"I didn't think you noticed."

"I always notice you, Delany." The warmth in his eyes present in their first dance was back.

"Did you see John Crawley?"

Field glanced quickly around. "No, not yet."

"Sarah says he's following the governor around."

A look of disgust crossed his features.

"My sentiments exactly," Delany said as they passed through to their new position.

Field escorted her back to the table and the waiting Sarah. She had no sooner picked up her glass than Isaac offered his hand for the next dance. Three couples down was John Crawley and Hester Morgan.

"Delany, I would like to ask you if I may come to see you sometime soon."

It would be an interesting evening. How had she managed to forget Isaac Harrison?

"We're friends, Isaac. You can come see me anytime you wish," she told him as she passed through to the other side of the line. "Bring your mother with you, and we can have a long visit." She smiled at him with what she hoped he knew was a strictly friendly way.

He was silent as he walked her back to Sarah and Field.

"Mrs. Fleet." John Crawley wiped his hands down the front of his coat, carefully avoiding the red plumage affixed to his lapel, and offered a short bow.

"Mr. Crawley, we did not expect to see you here."

"It is a wonder, is it not? I came because Lord Dunmore asked me to attend him here." He passed a white handkerchief over his slick face.

"How do you leave Norfolk?"

"Still intact, though one cannot say for how long. Lord Dunmore grows weary of the so-called patriots."

Delany bristled. *Perhaps the patriots grow weary of Lord Dunmore.*

Field stepped closer to her side and took her elbow.

"Crawley, isn't it?" Field looked down from his height to the small man.

"Mr. Archer, Lord Dunmore has heard you are here. He would very much like to see you."

"Mr. Crawley," Sarah interrupted, "how is your dear mother?"

Crawley's face reddened. "My mother is ever in good health," he said.

Delany got the distinct impression he wished it weren't true.

The fiddler struck the bow, and Field stuck out his hand.

They moved through the dance smoothly. His

intimate smile met her at every turn and when they were done, he put her hand on his arm and escorted her to the opposite end of the hall where Simon and Hester stood.

"Delany Fleet," Hester declared, "I just heard you're the great emancipator. Freed all your slaves when Mr. Fleet died." Hester's chocolate brown eyes glittered. "Have you never heard that passage that says if you are a slave you should obey your masters with sincerity of heart?"

Delany's anger rose and stiffened her spine. Of course she was very well acquainted with the passages commonly used to promote slavery in the colony. She closed her eyes for two blinks. "How about, 'If you were called a slave? Don't worry about it; but if you are able to also become free, rather do that.' If God says it's better for us to be free, how can I in good conscience be anyone's master?"

"What else would you expect from an indentured servant. Would you have us free all the servants?" Hester jeered, her hard eyes challenging Field who stood behind her shoulder. Several guests circled the small group to hear the exchange. "You're as bad as Lord Dunmore."

"'The wind blows where it wishes,'" Delany countered, "'and you hear the sound of it, but do not know where it comes from and where it is going; so is everyone that is born of the Spirit.' How can someone follow the true calling of the Lord if he is slave?"

"Enough," Field commanded.

Delany could not read the scowl on his face.

Hester beamed triumphantly.

When Crawley was involved, she could see his protectiveness of her, but when Hester was the culprit, it seemed his loyalty was divided. No matter, she was used to taking care of herself, and she would again. He would be gone in just a couple of days now that the cargo had been donated to the militia. It was time to get used to being on her own again. Delany cast about for Sam and Molly. "If you will excuse me." She exited the group and headed for her family.

~*~

"Delany," Field called in a hoarse whisper.

He followed her, accompanied by the Fleets, out of the assembly room into the night. She didn't slow down. What was the matter with the woman? Didn't she hear him? "Delany," he called once more as they neared the wagon.

"What?" She turned on him so suddenly that they nearly collided.

"What happened back there?"

"Look." She moved away from Sam and Molly toward a tall oak. "Whatever this is that has been going on between us will end in a couple of days when you leave, so let's just drop it."

His heart plummeted. She was right. He would leave in a couple of days, but he had hoped to bring her with him. "Delany." He reached for and she allowed him to take her hand. "Simon Morgan is my friend." She pulled on her hand, but he held it firmly.

"But Horsey Hester doesn't mean a thing to me."

She snorted in recognition of the old name. "Then why did you…" Her eyes widened. "You don't agree with me on slavery." She forcefully withdrew her hand.

"It's complicated."

"No, it isn't. You either agree with me that all men have a right to be free or you don't."

Archer Hall and its hundreds of dependents flitted through his mind. The plantation belonged to his father. Even if he did agree, he could do nothing to rectify the situation. How did she miss the fact that he couldn't just turn loose on society hundreds of men, women, and children to fend for themselves? They needed shelter and food. How were they to provide for themselves if he were to turn them all out on a whim? "Delany, it isn't as simple as that."

"Yes, it is." She turned from him and climbed into the back of Sam's wagon.

He followed them home with an empty wagon. She was right in one respect. Now that the firelocks were delivered, he could go home. He didn't need her to pass through as himself with no cargo. He was free to leave.

Who would protect her while she finished preparing her house? Sam couldn't spare the time or the labor. Ruben had his hands full with Mary and the baby.

Delany wasn't his problem. She'd made it clear that she preferred for him to leave, and that's just what he would do. He would have Robert pack him at first light.

~*~

Drizzle obscured the morning. Field had laid awake most of the night wrestling with his thoughts. At some point, he must have slept. He knew that only because he'd wakened to the sound of the children playing on the stairs. He dressed and went in search of his man who had been making himself handy around the farm of late.

The family remained inside due to the rain. Sam in his office, the children scattered around Molly as she attempted to keep them occupied.

"Where is Delany?" Field asked Molly.

"She's at Button Cove. She left early this morning to begin removing some of her things."

A cold fear threaded through his gut.

"She went there alone?"

"Mr. Archer, Delany has been on her own for a long time. She knows how to take care of herself. Besides, the Seldons should arrive today."

The Seldons' impending arrival made him feel a little better but not good enough to release the fear that clenched his insides. She would be furious with him if he interfered, but he couldn't leave until he knew she was safe. The thought of her alone at that house didn't sit well with him at all.

23

Glad that the sun didn't have the gall to shine this morning, Delany made her way slowly to Button Cove on squishy ground. She'd slept badly. She hoped the Seldons didn't make it in the rain. She wasn't in the mood to be nice or cheerful to anyone.

It was officially over. Her heart withered under the declaration.

It had been in front of her eyes the whole time. She'd been so blind. So busy focusing on his amber eyes and the red glint in his hair that she'd missed the most glaring incompatibility of all. They could never make anything of the feelings that she now thought they shared. It was a matter of principle. She would never own another person, and she couldn't be married to one who did either. According to Field's declaration last night, she could only conclude that he disagreed and would continue to run Archer Hall the way it had always been run—on the backs of slaves. She would have no part of it.

Delany stabled her horse and saw to his needs before entering her house. Inside was dark and hollow. She lit the fire already laid in the fireplace in the parlor and sat on the couch.

The crackle of the fire was the only sound inside. Delany gazed into the flames and saw her life stretch out before her, quiet and gray. She would miss the shop and its customers and artisans. Mr. Clayton, a shipwright with fingers as thick as cigars, who made clever wooden puzzle boxes in his spare time. The widow Blankenship, a lady with a sharp tongue and knack for making doll clothes. She would miss them.

It hadn't been a wise move to come here to wait without her work basket. There wasn't even a scrap of paper in the house so she could write a letter to Mr. Harris. She needed to instruct him to close her house and send specific items and effects on to her here.

The Seldons were to arrive within the hour. She would give them two. If they hadn't arrived by then, she would go home to Molly's. The colorful sounds of the children would comfort her heart.

Her heart stopped when the door opened and boots scraped across the wooden hallway.

"Delany."

"Field. Death by fright is not how I wish to get to heaven."

He took her hands into his own. "And how do you wish to get to heaven, my dear," His teasing grin was perilously close. The electricity between them pulled her toward his lips and another kiss. She shook her head and stepped back.

"I will not go to heaven with you ever again."

"So, you admit—"

Was that triumph registering in his arrogant amber eyes?

"I admit nothing."

He challenged her with a look.

"I will admit that I have thought that I was in love with you. There can be no shame in that any longer."

Astonishment rose on his face.

"It's no secret. I was infatuated with you as a child." She cast her eyes down at the admission.

He stepped forward, no doubt to take her in his arms again.

"Stop," she ordered.

His movement suspended like a clockwork toy, bewilderment on his features. How she loved that face, the teasing look of conspiracy in his eyes, the intimate smile he'd shared with her and no one else. He was open with her, like a little boy, and like a little boy, his heart was visible to her. She longed to reach up and caress his cheek and feel his lips on her own again.

"Am I allowed to speak?"

She took a deep breath. "Yes." If she was to do what she must, she must hear him. He deserved a chance to say his piece. Then, as she walked that gray corridor that was to be her life, she would know that she had been fair to him.

"Delany Button, I love you." The words she had dreamed to hear tasted like burnt pudding. He approached her again and took her hands and held them to his chest. "I wish to marry you."

The brittle steel in her back cracked. "I cannot marry a man who owns other people."

Frustration blew the breath from him. He dropped her hands. "It's just not that simple." He strode to the window and braced his hands on either side, back facing her. "It's illegal to free slaves. I admit it was ingenious for you to pay them so they could buy their freedom." He swung around to face her. "How do I do that with hundreds?"

"It is simple. It's not easy, but it's simple," she countered.

His broad shoulders sagged.

"This is what it's to be?" The amber of his eyes darkened to a muddy brown. "I have searched every country looking for you," he stormed. "I found you here, under my nose all this time. You, who are born and bred of this place, cannot live with me on its terms?"

The steel forged and strengthened once more. "I am not born of this place. I was brought here as a servant."

He stilled at her declaration.

"I am still a servant to the only One who never left me. The One who sent His Son to die for me. He has my allegiance, and I will not betray Him for you or anyone else."

He took her hands once more. "What will I do without you?"

"You will do what you have always done. Live and breathe and farm. Maybe someday you will find someone else."

Muddy brown turned to brown pebbles. He closed and she could no longer see his heart.

"I shall leave for the Morgans' home directly." He walked down the hallway and out of the house.

Tears dripped from her chin. He was gone this time, and he would never come back. Grief tore through her midsection. She found the couch and lay sobbing. What would she do without him? When she was a child, she'd loved as a child. She knew this was no fleeting affection. She would never be the same. She coiled into a ball. How could this happen? *Why would You let me love him so?* she screamed upward and then punched the couch. If there was patience in the silence, she didn't feel it. Pounding the couch with her fists was surprisingly helpful. She dealt a final blow and sat up. She didn't wish to be found by the Seldons this way. Delany glanced at her clock.

The Seldons were overdue.

On the ride home, a clear blue patch of sky was visible in the north.

"Mr. Archer isn't here," Molly informed her when she sat at the desk in the parlor. Delany pulled Christopher into her lap after he raised his hands. The boy wrapped his chubby little arms around her neck and squeezed. Her spirits lifted a shade. These little arms were better than any tonic for her black mood. "Has he left for the Morgans' home?" Her deceitful heart betrayed her and deflated at the news.

"He hasn't taken his leave of me, so I don't think so. Delany, what has happened?" Molly put her arm around Delany's shoulder. "Have you parted ways?"

Constriction built in her throat. She nodded her ascent. "I refused him."

Molly's eyebrows furrowed and creased her otherwise smooth forehead. "Why? I thought you loved him."

"You know why."

"I've heard the Archers are exceptional owners; they never beat their slaves. They are treated well there, Delany."

"I stand by my position. No one should own another person. It doesn't matter if you treat them nicely. They are not free to be who God intended them to be."

"You know I agree with you, but you have to make allowances for people to grow. Not everything is black and white."

"This is."

Delany hadn't fully recovered when Isaac Harrison strode into the room wearing a black suit that accented his wide shoulders.

Molly raised her eyebrows at Delany and stood to greet their guest.

"Welcome, Mr. Harrison. I believe Mr. Fleet is in his office."

"Thank you, Mrs. Fleet, but I came to see the other Mrs. Fleet."

This day was going from bad to worse. He'd clearly missed her message about friendship last night.

Isaac turned to Delany. "The day has turned quite fine. Would you care to take a walk with me?"

No, I would rather sit here and write a letter to my attorney. "Of course." She stood, hoping that her black mood would not leak out and damage their friendship.

Once they'd reached the porch, he offered his arm. Delany placed her hand on his strong arm wishing it was Field's. They walked past the dependencies and out toward the lane. They headed in the opposite direction of Button Cove.

"Delany, I am sure you must have surmised why I've come to talk to you."

What could she say to that? You've come here so that I can break your heart?

"Isaac, I'm—"

"It's my mother."

"What?" A little spark of sunshine peeked out of her worry. Sarah was bright and cheerful last night. Nothing drastic could have happened in the small time they'd been apart.

"You are my mother's very best friend, and I know she will listen to you."

"What's the matter with your mother?"

"She's forsaken her widow's black and is dressing like a woman half her age. I think she's hunting for a husband."

Delany laughed.

"This is not a laughing matter, Delany. My mother is not a young woman. She has some money to live on, and I am worried that someone will take advantage of her."

"Is there anyone in particular you are worried about?"

"No. That's the problem. There is not one particular gentleman. She's acting like a girl fresh out of the schoolroom. If there was someone in particular, I could look into it and determine suitability. As it is, she is running about willy-nilly."

"I know you will forgive me if I speak too freely."

"Of course. I've come for your advice and intervention, if necessary. You needn't spare my feelings."

"Isaac, you must agree that your mother has her own free will, and she can do with her life as she pleases."

"That goes without saying. Of course, she can do as she wishes. I only want what's best for her. Most people remarry within a few months of widowhood."

"You haven't," she prodded.

"Neither have you."

"I haven't a need to. Tom left me well off and..." She let the thought trail off. She couldn't tell him that now she was in love with someone she could never have.

"I loved Polly. We grew up together, and there just isn't anyone else for me."

"Have you told your mother that?"

"What does that have to do with anything?"

"Your mother has been a widow for five years. What do you think has caused this sudden change?"

"You think she's trying to force me to marry?"

"I think she might want you to feel free to marry, which is a very different thing altogether."

He took a deep breath and exhaled. "When will people get it through their heads that when and if I wish to marry, I will take care of it myself?"

"I promise I will go see her, but I think you'd better have a talk with her yourself."

~*~

Field watched Delany stroll with Harrison from the top of the small ridge that crested to the east of the road. It didn't take long for her to move on. Is that what she meant by him finding someone else? Had she found someone that quickly? Harrison had been hovering around since they'd arrived at the Fleets' home.

Once he'd seen her safely home from her house, he'd ridden farther to stretch his horse and himself. The ride had done nothing to relieve his tension. He would have to leave soon. If it was next to impossible to watch her walk with Harrison, it would be downright unbearable to see her give herself to him in marriage.

The sky opened up a squall just as he arrived in the barn. The rain would set him back a day or two while the roads dried, but it wouldn't keep him from going to the Morgans' home.

24

A groom met Field in the Morgans' barn. He'd handed the reins over and headed to the house when he caught sight of Hester's chestnut hair behind the walls of a stall. She wore a plain muslin gown, her hair hung in a long braid down her back. Minus the cages of fashion, she was as small as a schoolgirl.

"Hester, I'd forgotten I should expect to see you in a barn."

She sniffled and turned to face him. "Field, I'm sure we didn't expect to see you today in all this rain." She spoke carefully as though she weighed every word.

"No. I just rode over. Thought I'd spend a couple of days before I head home. Simon is expecting me."

"Of course, you are most welcome. You will find Simon with my uncle in the library." She turned back toward her horse and continued brushing the sorrel coat.

He resumed his path to the house.

"Field," she called.

He faced her.

"I believe I owe you an apology."

"How so?"

"You needn't be kind. My brother gave me quite a dressing down last night." She kept her hand on the back of the horse as she made her way around to the other side while murmuring reassuring words to the large animal. "It seems that you are to be congratulated, and I am to keep my 'disdainful comments' to myself."

"It's hard to imagine…"

"What? My scholarly brother raising his voice?" she laughed. "That's probably why he got away with it. I was absolutely stunned into silence at first." She stepped away from her horse, "My apology must be for Mrs. Fleet but also for you." Her gaze slipped from him to the open barn door and back again, "My comments were rude and unfeeling, and I am sorry for them."

He accepted her apology and quickly made for the house.

"For what am I to be congratulated?" Field asked Simon after they had settled in the back parlor alone.

"I assume you shall be engaged to Delany Fleet in the very near future if you are not already."

Field closed his eyes and breathed deep. "Am I that obvious?"

"It won't come as a surprise to those who truly know you. You've been sweet on her since we were kids."

"Have I?"

"Did you think all that talk of her being a servant fooled me? She followed you around, and you let her. There's only one reason for that."

Field felt blood tinge his ears. "She refused me."

"What did you do to her?"

"What do you mean?" Frustration rose. "I've done nothing. You heard the crux of her argument in the altercation with Hester. Thank you, by the way."

Simon nodded and rested back in his chair, legs open, hands resting on the arms. It was his professorial pose. "I came in late, just in time to hear my sister deride Delany for being a servant."

"Her issue is with slavery. She will not own any and will not marry someone who owns them either."

"Technically you don't own any," Simon supplied.

"It doesn't signify because I will inherit Archer Hall and its servants."

"True."

"So, while I don't own any slaves, I will, and so she will not have me." Saying the words out loud made the bleak truth more real. His heart cried out, "Do something," but all he could do was study the carpet at Simon's feet.

"So that's that." Simon's abrupt tone snapped Field's attention. "You'll walk away, just like that."

"What else can I do? I'm a gentleman. I cannot force her, I would not."

"Don't be a fool. What are your other options?"

"I can't just release all my slaves. They'll starve. Whole families turned out, nowhere to go..."

"It's something we will all have to come to terms with."

This turn in the conversation did not surprise him. Simon was a scientist and philosopher. "This nation is being built on the very idea that England is making slaves of us with their oppressive laws. We are building a nation of free men. How can we not free them?"

Field kept his gaze on his friend. "The patriots are outraged at Dunmore's threat to free the slaves. It has made him most unpopular," Field countered.

"So I hear daily from my uncle. I can afford to be objective for I, like you, have not come into my inheritance. I've been thinking of what to do about it."

"We cannot just turn them out. Not only is it illegal, they would starve. And we need their labor."

Simon contracted in his chair to sit up straight, fingers woven together across his spare stomach. "That assumes that you agree freeing them is the path we must follow."

Field stood at the crossroads. The words of that minister, Wesley, whispered in his ears. *"Liberty is the right of every human creature...and no human law can deprive him of that right..."* He knew in an instant that required no further thought than freedom was the right course of action. "I think we must." As he said it, his conviction grew. *How could it be otherwise?* A burden he didn't realize he'd carried lifted from his shoulders.

"It must be possible, if we look at it mathematically, to release them in such a way as to benefit us both."

"Fleet has done it, but he told me himself he only had eight when he freed them. How do I free hundreds?"

"We shall put our minds to it and find a way. During the meantime, you can live at Button Cove with Mrs. Fleet."

Joy spread through him. Of course, he could live at Button Cove. He would have to speak to his father and mother about the dispensation of the slaves and the land, but if they did it well, it could work.

Field spent the next few days with the Morgans talking politics, riding when he could, and wrestling with ways to approach Delany. Simon had been right, of course. He'd always been fond of Delany even as she'd followed him around on the farm.

He missed her. The longer he stayed away, the more he knew he could not go home without her. Would she accept him without his worldly possessions? Would she compromise until the land was in his power and he could set things right?

25

The last of Delany's trunks were loaded onto the wagon.

Sam, Ruben, and Freewill followed on horseback.

Molly and the children rode in a wagon.

It was Delany's big day. She was finally moving into Button Cove. The Seldons had sent a note. Rain and sickness delayed them no longer. They would arrive by the end of the week. Pauline had agreed to cook until the Seldons arrived.

To finally be in her own home once again was a welcome blessing. Delany had been too long at Sam and Molly's. She wanted her own food and her own bed. Her own schedule. Here she could move around without bruising her heart by bumping into memories of Field at every turn.

"Aunt Delany, can I stay here with you?" Margaret, holding onto her doll, Peg, slipped her hand into Delany's.

Delany remained speechless. The flames of the fireplace and the gray stretches of her life loomed.

"Margaret, Aunt Delany has just arrived. She is not situated yet. She may not wish for company on her very first night," Molly said.

"Quite the contrary, Molly. I would be delighted if Margaret spent the night here with me."

Molly's eyes widened. "Very well, but you must send her home the minute she gets underfoot."

Delany and Margaret stood hand in hand watching the wagons leave for the Fleet farm. She was home.

Pauline stood off to the side.

"Well, what should we have for dinner?"

Pauline looked as surprised as Margaret at the question. "It's late in the day, Miss Delany."

"Don't worry, Pauline. I thought we could have ham and biscuits in the kitchen."

A blustery wind scraped some scattered leaves across the bricks.

"Can we have cake?" Margaret nearly jumped up and down but caught herself.

Delany grinned. "Only if Pauline has time to make one. We don't have much of anything around here since we just moved in."

"Of course. I forgot that."

"I'll take a look, Miss Margaret, and see if Betsy made us a cake." Pauline grinned at the child.

"While Pauline makes supper, I have something to show you."

Margaret's face lit with excitement.

The trunk Delany sought was placed in the extra bedroom across the hall from her own. She motioned to Margaret to kneel beside her in front of the massive chest and lifted the lid.

"What is all this?"

"Sometimes, in the shop, we get a particularly fine bolt of cloth, but if we don't sell it all, I save the leftover bits."

Margaret audibly inhaled her enthusiasm. "What are they for?"

"What else?" Delany stuck her hands down in the trunk and pulled up several scraps of shining cloth. "Doll clothes."

Margaret took the offered material with wide eyes. "Can we?"

"Of course. Pick out what you like. There is lace and ribbon in here, too."

Margaret set to organizing what she found by size and color.

Delany dug down the side to find the patterns she had stuck there. "When you've decided, meet me downstairs in the dining room."

After gathering scissors, pins, and thread, Delany headed to the dining room and the only large enough work surface in the house.

Margaret joined her with a selection of a delicate gold silk and matching ecru lace. She had a good eye for color. It would match the coloring of her raven-haired Peg very well.

Margaret had the sandy-brown coloring and warm brown eyes of her mother. Consequently, she always seemed to be dressed in some shade of blue. Blue suited her, but the change of gold for her Peg, who was also always dressed in blue, made Delany wonder what other changes the girl would make if given the chance.

Margaret picked the simplest pattern of the five that Delany had available.

"Good choice. We might even get it finished before you have to go home tomorrow."

They had finished cutting out the pieces when Pauline came in with a large tray of thickly sliced ham and warm biscuits.

"That smells delicious." Delany directed Pauline to place the tray on the empty half of the table. She retrieved three plates from the sideboard and placed them in front of three chairs.

Delany sat at the head of the table and beckoned Margaret and Pauline to her right and left.

Pauline stopped with hands on the back of her chair. "Do you mean for me to sit down with you, Miss Delany?"

"Yes, of course. You are most welcome to sit with us while we eat this wonderful smelling meal you have prepared."

Pauline stiffly moved the chair and sat, hands in her lap, head down, on the very edge of her seat.

Delany reached across, laying her hand flat on the table. "There are no slaves in this house, Pauline. Only servants of God."

"Betsy says she's ate at the table in the big house with the master, but I never believed it, not really."

"I understand why you wouldn't." Delany blushed when her stomach growled.

Margaret laughed.

"I think that says it all. Let's eat."

Margaret prayed for the food while they all

bowed.

Delany passed the plate of biscuits to Margaret and asked Pauline to pass the ham.

Dinner continued in near silence as the three of them satisfied their appetites.

Delany rose to stack the dinner plates when they were done eating.

"I'll carry them out, Miss Delany."

"It's no trouble for us to help."

"If you'll pardon me, Miss, you stay here, and I will bring back the cake." Her broad face crinkled in a wide smile at Margaret.

"There's cake!" A little jump escaped Margaret that time.

Delany and Pauline laughed.

"I'll be right back."

Delany and Margaret finished cutting out the pieces and prepared to retire to the parlor. Delany lit the fire that had already been laid while Margaret brought in the little dress.

Pauline arrived with cake, and the three shared it in the parlor in front of the fire. As Delany and Margaret commenced their sewing, Pauline excused herself to the kitchen.

26

Isaac's house was larger than Delany expected. Fully as large as her own, it had a symmetrical face and a gambrel roof.

In the parlor, Sarah enveloped her in warm hug.

Unexpected tears clouded Delany's vision and clogged her throat.

Sarah held her tighter. "What's wrong?"

"It's a long story." Delany stepped away and wiped her eyes. "One I didn't plan on telling you today." She choked on a smile.

"Tell me anyway." Sarah patted the settee cushion next to her.

Delany took her seat and, once again, described her feelings for Field. "I truly thought I was safe. The infatuation of a young girl is so much fairy dust. It gets wiped away with the cloth of time."

"Very poetic."

"Yes, well I might be feeling a little dramatic. But having him here has been a very real mistake." Delany stood to pace, worrying her hands in the process. "There was nothing else to do. I could not turn him away. I could not help but fall in love with him. And I could not accept him when he offered."

Sarah sat quiet and still.

"How can you just sit there?" Delany spat.

"I am listening to you."

"What do I do?"

Sarah looked at her hands and then raised her gaze to Delany. "You pray."

Delany tried not to roll her eyes. Surely, she could do more than that.

"Have you asked God what you should do?" Calm and serene, Sarah went on. "I can't help but believe that God brought him to you for a reason."

The look in his eyes after the visit from Craig Reid interrupted her thoughts. Field changed that day. Perhaps that was why the Lord had brought him to her. She'd allowed her foolish, worldly self to get in the way. She'd been so selfish. "Isaac wanted me to speak to you."

"Oh?" A conspiratorial gleam shone in Sarah's eyes. "Just what did he want you to talk to me about?"

"All this," Delany gestured to Sarah's dress. Today she wore a silk brocade gown of midnight blue with a mustard yellow petticoat. The ensemble took ten years off her friend. Delany wasn't sorry to see the change. "You look splendid, but Isaac is worried about you. He says you are running around like a girl fresh from the schoolroom."

"So, he noticed, did he?" Sarah adjusted her skirts and added, "Well, it's about time, too."

"Are you trying to let Isaac know that he is free to marry?"

"No. He knows that. I want him to know that I am

free to marry."

The light began to dawn in Delany's mind, "So you think that he doesn't think he has to marry because you are here to take care of the womanly things he needs done."

"Precisely. As long as I am here to care for Lucy and run his household for him, he's content."

"Are you sure? You only came to live here a couple of weeks ago."

"He and his brothers have been pestering me to come live with him ever since poor Polly died." She cast a derisive grin. "Lord Dunmore succeeded where my children failed. Well, I'm not having it."

"Surely, you can't mean to coerce him."

"No, that wouldn't work. And I wouldn't do it anyway, but neither will I stay here to raise his daughter and run his household."

Her vehemence surprised Delany. "What brought this on, Sarah? You love Lucy."

Sarah's hands fisted in her lap. "In truth, I cannot tell you. Robert was a good man. He was good to me, but he didn't love me."

Delany knew what that was like.

"You told me once that you were a rich widow who didn't need a husband." Sarah took Delany's hand. "Well, I may not be rich, but I'm comfortable, and I'm not interested in anyone running my life anymore. Not Isaac; not anyone."

"How does finding a new husband help you? I would think the opposite."

"That, my dear, depends on the man." Sarah

grinned and patted Delany's hand. "But that is neither here nor there. I will accomplish my goal when Isaac marries again."

There was no arguing any further. Sarah had decided, and Sarah would stay the course. Her serene friend had showed her stubborn side before. Once she dug in, one might as well try to add an inch to one's height. It just wouldn't happen.

"Have you ever thought about gray areas, Delany?" Sarah switched topics.

"Yes, in the practical application of truth sometimes there are gray areas. And some are black and white. Lies are always wrong, and so is slavery."

"How many slaves does he have?"

"I've no idea—hundreds, maybe."

"Have you also figured out how he's supposed to go about this emancipation?"

"He would have to agree that it was the right course to take before he made such plans as that. He didn't agree. He asked me to live here on 'those terms.' That's someone who won't change the status quo."

"Delany, you have to allow for growth to happen at its own pace."

"I'm not interested in waiting around for someone to come to his senses. I'm removing to Button Cove and will forget I ever knew Field Archer."

The sky had clouded over while they'd visited. One glance out of the window told Delany she'd better be on her way or get stuck in a storm. She collected Pauline and embraced her friend.

Two miles away from Isaac's house, Delany

shivered in the newly chilled wind. Neither one of them had brought along a cloak. The day had been so fine when they'd left. A strong gust pushed them along the path. Her horse balked at the rustle of the branches and the snow of leaves released in the blow. She glanced back to see Pauline shivering in the light homespun dress she wore. She pulled off the jacket of her brown velvet riding habit and passed it to Pauline as soon as she caught up.

"Are you sure, Miss?" Pauline asked.

Delany nodded agreement. She still had velvet sleeves to cover her arms. Hopefully, the rain would hold off. They didn't need to catch their death out here. Besides, she needed to do something nice for the woman. Pauline had worked beside her to turn the house into Button Cove. She would speak to Molly about it. Perhaps a couple of new dresses and a cloak for winter would be a blessing.

They were half way home when thunder struck and a hard driving rain laced with pea-sized hail pelted them.

Delany was thankful for the full brimmed hat wilting over her face. It didn't help with visibility, but it did help keep the rain from directly hitting her eyes.

They slowed to a walk.

The last time she'd been this cold, Field wrapped her in his coat. The warmth of his body was enough for the two of them. Her withered heart made the cold worse. It would be just so good to be wrapped up in his coat right now and feel the warmth of his love for her.

There was no sound but the thrumming rain. The trees were gray sticks blending into the dense curtain of water. As they rounded the curve in the lane, a tall, dark man stepped out into the road. At this distance, it could be Freewill or his brother, George. If it was Freewill, she would rejoice. His brother George sent rivulets of fear through her nearly frozen body.

Freewill was a large spirited man, always able to find the good in any situation he encountered. George was a man denied. Even when she'd freed him, he could do nothing but sneer that it was "about time" before running off.

Her rifle lay in its holster soaking wet like everything else. It wouldn't be much use until it dried out.

"Miss Delany," the man called out as she approached.

Lord keep us safe and get us home.

"Why, George, it's been a very long time." She gripped the reigns tighter as they approached him. "I'm sorry we can't stop in this storm. Pauline and I need to get home before we catch our death in this weather."

His head came to her shoulders. He grabbed the reins from her hands as pretty-as-you-please with no warning. It happened so fast Delany didn't respond.

"It's time, Pauline," George called out behind them.

Pauline nodded to George.

"Time for what, George?"

"You'll see. Right now, you're coming with me.

The boss wants to see you real bad."

George led her off the trail long enough to retrieve his own horse. He mounted all the while keeping Delany in tow. They started back down the path. She looked back at Pauline.

The girl's face was hard as she pointed a finger forward.

Delany waited until they'd come around the bend. If she guessed right, she was close to Button Cove. They wouldn't expect her to go there. She could hide there until the rain let up and then make it to Sam and Molly. Right in the middle of the turn when she'd lost sight of Pauline, she slipped out of her saddle and began to run through the woods. The thump of the key against her thigh as she ran was her only comfort.

The footpath she'd known as a girl was easy to find. It was smarter to stay off the path, but she didn't dare risk getting lost. The woods ended at the garden at the back of Button Cove. Though overgrown with vines and other weeds, it didn't provide the cover that made her comfortable. There was no sign of George or Pauline. But she couldn't think about that until she was behind the locked door of her house. Hopefully, they would think she'd head straight to Sam and Molly's.

A short set of brick stairs led her up to the backyard of the house. Dependencies lined either side of the path up to the house. She was soaked to the skin. There was no one here to greet her, but there would be. Before too long, there would be. Soon there would be fires and good food and—she stopped. There wouldn't be little chubby arms and brown eyes to greet her.

Thanking God for the small number of stores she had already had delivered to the kitchen, she trudged up the stairs to her home. Her sodden dress was as heavy as a stuffed hogshead. She couldn't wait to get it off and put on something dry.

She opened the door and stepped inside. Silence rang in her ears. The door should not have been open. She was sure she'd locked both doors before she left. Her key still rested in her pocket. There was the extra key hanging on its hook beside the door. No matter. No doubt it was just some oversight. She locked the door and rested her head against the solid wood.

"I'll take the key if you don't mind." The fake polish of Josiah Philips's voice echoed in the bare ballroom.

Instant fire straightened Delany. She turned to face the intruder standing in the hallway door. "How dare you enter my house."

"Oh, I think you will find me very daring, Mrs. Fleet." Waves of cold evil reached her.

"Get out of my house now."

He took slow steps toward her, boots clicking with each step. "I'm not going anywhere, Delany. Do you mind if I call you that? Delany?" He reached her and rolled a tendril of her hair between his thumb and forefinger. "You're soaking wet."

She jerked her head away from his hand and sidestepped.

He grabbed the hand with the key and crushed. "Give me the key."

She attempted to roll her hand to free it from his

grip.

He bent it back until it would break. The key clanged to the floor. He threw her to her knees. "Now pick it up and hand it to me."

Lord, please help me. Delany retrieved the key and stood.

"Give it to me nicely, or I will break your hand." He smiled at her.

She fought against the revulsion. Back straight, she handed him the key, hoping that the importance of this key would mask the other key she still had in her pocket.

"What do you want?"

"It's not what I want. It's what the boss wants. He'll tell you when he comes." A wicked light shone in his black eyes. He stepped around her with an appraising gaze.

"I'm going to my room." She headed toward the hallway. It was then she realized they were not alone. George and Pauline were there with the two men who had captured Field.

"Take a good look, gentlemen. This is the ghostly Grace Sherwood." He chuckled.

The men hardened into standing up straight.

"Don't let her humiliate you again."

They jeered at her. "Won't happen again, boss."

Delany lifted her chin and passed by them.

Pauline did not look her in the eye.

George's hard eyes never left hers.

"Put on your finest gown. I expect to see you in fifteen minutes."

Delany didn't turn back to argue. She would be down when she was done. She was glad to get a few minutes in her room alone. And she really did need to get out of her wet clothes. She didn't have many grand gowns, but she thought she might have brought one that would suit his odd request and her own needs.

The bedroom door did not have a lock. Out the window was a sheer drop of two stories. There was no roof, and she had no rope. She was stranded a mile and a half from her family. Sam and Molly would think that she'd stayed with Isaac and Sarah, and Sarah would think she'd made it home. It was perfect. No one knew she was missing.

Who was "the boss"? And what could he want with her? It was a pretty bold thing to hold a person hostage in her own home. What coward had the guts for that? Philips was here, but he wouldn't do anything. If he was ever caught, he'd hang. Who else would risk hanging to hold her here?

The horizon was hidden behind the curtain of rain that continued to beat down. Was Field out there? No. She was no longer his problem. He would not be watching for her safety any longer. She was alone. She needed to find a way out of the house. It was a little over a mile to the Fleets, but she could easily make it on foot if she could just get out of the house.

From the windows that overlooked the back of the house, Delany could see Philips' men standing in the doorways of the storehouse and the kitchen. They must have hidden when she passed by a few minutes ago. The only way would be out the front. If she could get to the stand of woods that separated the two Fleet properties unseen, she could make it to Molly's.

She dressed in blue silk and her warmest woolen petticoat. She wrapped a thick blue woolen shawl around her shoulders and tucked the key back into her pocket. On her feet, she placed her best pair of leather walking boots. They did look out of place with her silk, but if he asked, she would tell him it was for the warmth they offered. In truth, she had been bone-cold since she'd arrived home.

27

Night had fallen when Delany returned downstairs. She went immediately to the newly-made fire in the parlor. It wasn't hot enough yet to warm the room.

"I didn't give you permission to stand by that fire."

The cold menace of his words hit her from across the room. Fear shivered up her spine. She spun around to face him. "This is my home, Mr. Philips. I don't need your permission."

In two strides, she could smell his foul breath, feel the warmth of it on the tip of her nose, "You'll do what I say." His hand coiled around her arm and squeezed before he pushed her toward the couch across the room.

Delany righted herself.

"Take off your boots."

A gasp left her lips before she could restrain herself. It was not possible to remove her boots without being decidedly unladylike. She had no desire to expose any parts of her person to Josiah Philips.

"Take 'em off, or I'll make sure you can't walk." He pulled a pair of pliers from the pocket of his coat.

"Let me help you, Miss Delany." Pauline strode into the room, knelt before Delany, and helped her remove her boots.

Philips's face contorted in frustration. The evil light still shone from his black eyes.

Pauline rested back after the second boot came off and twisted to stand.

Philips's right hand slapped her as she rose.

Pauline hit the floor.

Delany came up off the couch.

"You interfere with me again and you won't be able to tell the tale."

George stepped between them before Philips struck again.

"You wanna hit somebody, you hit her." He pointed to Delany.

Delany froze. She wished she'd had a knife in her pocket instead of the key. Her scissors were in the work basket under the table just out of reach.

Philips grimaced. "Don't you tell me what to do, boy." He swung his fist again and struck George on the face. "You get outta here right now before I kill you."

The large black man shrank at the blow.

Delany moved to Pauline.

Then George unfolded himself into his full height, a head taller and two times broader than Philips. George swung his fist and connected with Philips' jaw.

Delany grabbed Pauline by the hand and headed for the door not waiting to discover whose bones she heard crack. The closest door led to the front of the house. Her heart pounded as she ran in slow motion dragging Pauline with her to safety.

Pauline pulled her hand free when they reached the ground outside. "I ain't leaving George here."

"George can take care of himself. We need to leave now." Delany could hear footsteps in the house. Mud squished up the sides of her stocking feet.

Pauline stood her ground.

Delany hitched up her skirts and ran toward the lane and Molly's house.

The moon hid behind storm clouds. The ground sucked at her feet as she ran. Small pebbles bruised her soft soles. It was cold, but she could make it to Sam and Molly if she wasn't followed. She didn't dare slow down to glance back. She prayed for rain. She hadn't run this much since she was a girl. Her side ached. Heart pounding loudly in her ears, she gasped for air. She had to catch her breath. Delany reached the sodden lane and ducked into the wood to rest against a tree. The field between the house and the lane was empty.

Philips did not follow.

Praise God. She prayed silently, trying to breathe through her nose to stifle the sound. A creak of leather, a snort. Someone was coming. Did she step out or wait until whoever it was passed? Delany had never felt fear like she had in that parlor with Josiah Philips and his pliers.

Surely, no one traveling on this road would be unfriendly to her. Stupid thought. Philips traveled by this road to get to her. Philips said he was waiting for his boss. Who was this boss and what did he want with her? No reason came to mind for why someone would want to kidnap her in her own home. She didn't even know anyone who knew Philips.

Mayhap it was Sam coming to check on her after the storm, in which case, she'd better stop him before he got there alone. One man couldn't stand against the five that traveled with Philips.

The rider was upon her position now. It could be the boss, but she couldn't take the risk that it was Sam.

Once again, she hitched up her skirts and walked out into the lane. She bounced right into a fat man.

"Why, is it Mrs. Fleet?"

Confused, Delany couldn't mistake the oily sound of John Crawley. At least he was someone she knew and could trust. He stood next to his horse in the muddy lane.

"Thank God you're here," she cried, grabbing onto his forearm. "I need to get home."

"Allow me to take you there. Are you all right?"

"No, I'm not all right. I should be very glad if you would just take me home. I will sort it out once I get there."

~*~

Restless feelings of dread invaded the evening. Field was worried about Delany. All was quiet when he rode by Button Cove this morning. The restlessness was probably due to rain trapping him in the house all afternoon. He'd made sure that he rode by her house twice a day since he'd been gone. Nothing had been amiss that he'd seen, but the house didn't rest easy with him.

The only thing he could see that he'd gained from the sojourn with his friends was that Hester had given up her pursuit of him. After their conversation in the barn, she'd been contrite. By dinner time the next day, her ability to flirt was on prime display. He was sure Simon was responsible for the haughty belligerence that arrived at breakfast the following morning and remained.

Tonight, she was again dressed in her own hair and a simple gown of rose silk.

Field thought she improved when she wasn't trying too hard to impress. She definitely wasn't for him, but someone was bound to love her someday. The conversation was lively as it always was with Mr. Morgan challenging his nephew while his wife admonished him. Field couldn't follow the thread. It had something to do with horse racing or maybe horse breeding. Whatever it was, it kept him thinking of the stable and how fast it would take him to saddle up. The rain had finally eased. Field stood to take his leave, startling the laughter that had commenced over what he didn't know. "I shall return shortly." He changed into his riding gear and headed for the barn.

Simon, dressed to ride, stood next to a stall while the groom saddled his horse.

"Something's wrong. I can feel it," Field told him.

"Where are we going?"

"Button Cove." Field's restlessness eased once he was astride Orion. They'd traveled the path to Button

Cove enough in the past few days that they should have no trouble finding their way. The mud was enough to make the toes squish but not enough for Orion to sink. They could be there in a flash, if it wasn't dark. They headed single file down the narrow road toward Button Cove.

The wind blew icy shafts down the neck of Field's overcoat.

Storm clouds closed the sky. Wet leaves slicked the ground.

"What do you expect?" Simon asked from behind.

"I don't know yet. All I know is that something is wrong, and I won't rest until I know she's all right."

28

"It's you." Delany spat around the swelling on the right side of her face. "You're the boss."

Crawley said nothing as he finished the knot between her wrists. He left a tail which he held with his free hand. With the other hand he towed the horse. He walked toward Button Cove.

"What do you want?"

"We'll talk all about that in the morning, my dear. Tonight, I want food and drink and sleep. I've had enough traipsing around after His Lordship."

"How could you send that fiend after me?"

He chuckled. "You mean Josiah? He's effective, my dear. People do what he tells them to do." He grinned with the sneer audible in his voice.

"I thought you were my friend."

He rounded and tugged her toward him. "My friend? You proved you were no friend of mine when you refused my hand."

Fear shivered down her spine.

"No more talk."

Delany complied and walked in step with him and the horse. Perhaps he would get lazy. If he did, she'd pull and run.

At the turn toward the front walk, his grip loosened and the rope slackened as he paid attention to turning the horse.

Delany turned to the right with all her might to yank the rope free.

Crawley yanked back.

Delany hit the muddy sand at his feet.

"Surely, you don't think I came all this way just to fail in my quest?" He chuckled again.

They arrived at the front door of Button Cove, Delany covered in mud. Her face ached from the first blow he'd given her in the road.

Philips' men met them at door.

Once inside, Crawley said, "Go to your room."

Rage stiffened her spine.

"I will not be ordered about in my own home."

"You'll do what I tell you, or you'll get another to match that growing on your face." He turned from her toward the men. "Untie the rope, and see Mrs. Fleet to her room. Post a guard outside the door."

Rubbing her wrists, she walked up the steps followed by the two jeering men whom she'd duped. Once in her room, she lit a candle and sat down on a wing-back chair.

There was nothing of much use in her room. Her workbasket was downstairs. At least she could get warm. What she would do to sit in a tub full of hot water. She removed the blue silk gown which was ruined by the mud and selected her muslin cleaning gown and the thickest pair of stockings she owned. Her boots were also downstairs. She chose the sturdiest of her everyday shoes adding serviceable buckles with no adornment. If she got another chance to run, she would be better prepared.

A small tap on the door and Pauline entered carrying a platter of food.

"What do you want, Pauline?"

Pauline placed the platter on the round table next to Delany's wing-back chair.

"They got George, Miss Delany. Them men is talking about hanging him."

"Because he hit Philips?"

"They're sayin' his jaw's broke." Pauline's face lit with hope.

What does she think I can do about it? Lord, please show me the way out of here. "Can you fetch me some water to wash with, please?"

"Yes'm."

Broken jaw. Served him right, but Pauline's concern was justified. If they thought he was guilty, they could hang him and no one would care. If only she could get to Sam and Molly. *If only Field were here.* Delany got up and paced the floor. There was no use in dwelling on what one couldn't have. The small courtyard of dependencies lay outside her window. The kitchen was well lit. She could imagine Pauline in there cooking her food for the invaders.

There was no sign of George.

She lay fully clothed on her bed listening to intruders in her home. Sleep came unbidden in the early hours of the morning.

~*~

John Crawley stood behind her desk. On its surface were some official looking documents. He came out from behind her desk and wiped his hands down the front of his coat. "Mrs. Fleet, I am in a forgiving mood this morning, so I've decided to give you one more chance."

Delany froze. A chance at what?

"I wish to marry you."

Her response was derisive laughter. "Are you serious? Do you really think I would marry a man who hit me in the face, paid someone to break my feet, and kept me a prisoner in my own home?"

Crawley shrugged. "I want Tom's property in Norfolk. Particularly the warehouse. I am willing to marry you to get it." He came close enough to touch her.

She stepped back.

"You will be cared for."

"It's my property."

Frustration registered on his features. "Don't let's quibble about trifles."

"It is no trifle to steal a person's property in word or deed."

He grabbed her arm and pulled her up against his chest. "My friend George tells me that you stand in that waterfall on your porch naked for all to see." John's obsidian eyes gleamed. Spittle dribbled down the growth at the corner of his mouth. "Is that what you like?" He placed his forefinger under her chin.

Shame heated her face. She'd been right. The shadow she'd seen in the kitchen was George. She held her head high. She would not show him her humiliation.

He slid his finger down her bodice.

"Don't touch me." She pulled from him and stood separate.

"I'm not leaving here without what I came for. If you won't marry me, then you can sell me the warehouse."

"No." She stepped back again and bumped into her desk.

Crawley closed the distance.

"I will turn Field Archer over to Lord Dunmore. The best he could hope for is to be pressed into His Majesty's service." When she turned her head at his fetid breath, he grabbed her chin and forced her to look at him. "Or he could be hanged for treason."

A wave of nausea washed over her senses. She would not allow harm to come to Field if she could prevent it.

"How much are you willing to pay?"

"I'll pay what you charged your slaves for freedom." Glee lit up his face. He thought he was clever. "One dollar."

"Don't be ridiculous," She pushed him off, feeling some of her power returning. This was a realm she knew about. Her warehouse was worth several thousand pounds. He knew her well enough to know she wouldn't give in that easily. She walked to the window. "My warehouse is worth far more—"

"What is his life worth to you? More than it's worth to His Majesty or Lord Dunmore, I assure you."

"I assume you came here with papers."

"You know me well, Delany." He leaned over the desk, found the relevant papers, and handed them to her.

Sure enough, there it was in writing. Her warehouse and shop to be sold for one dollar. Hands shaking, she gave them as careful a read as she could, given the unrest in her mind. Delany took the pen he offered and dipped it in the ink. She bent over her desk and signed away her property. The finality of it took her flailing gusto and dissipated it into the cold air. Would she always be at the mercy of such men?

Crawley, standing beside her, scooped up the paper as soon as she laid down the quill. He blew on the signature. Once he confirmed it was dry, he placed the paper in a folder in a leather case.

"You got what you want. Leave my house at once."

"Ah, but I haven't gotten all that I wanted." He grabbed her arms and held her in a vice-like grip. Her backside bumped into the desktop. "I noticed my books were missing from your library. Did you borrow them?" He stank of sweat, and his foul breath heated her cheek.

"Get off of me." She pushed.

He pushed her down on the desk. His weight pinned her down and cut off her breath.

"Get off!" She punched his arms, closing her eyes and praying for strength.

A thump rattled through Crawley. He groaned.

Delany saw stars when his head banged into her forehead. His body slumped, squeezing out the last of her air.

Brown hair tinged with red glowed in the morning sun. Field grabbed Crawley and threw him to the floor with force.

Delany righted herself on the desk in time to see Simon enter.

Crawley lay on the floor holding his head.

"Take over here, will you?"

Simon grinned. "With pleasure."

"Are you all right?" Field placed his hands on either side of her face.

Delany burrowed into the embrace as his arms encircled her. One hand slid up to caress her neck and scalp. "Just hold me safe."

He tightened his hold and kissed the top of her head.

Dear God, there has to be a way.

"Don't touch me." Crawley whined from the floor as Simon tapped him with a boot to get him up.

Delany laughed at the irony.

"I've got to get out of here." She went for the leather case, retrieved the signed document, and strode to the fireplace.

"You stay out of my things."

Delany laughed again. Anger surged her forward toward him while she held up the documents. "This is mine, and I shall do with it what I like." She threw the papers into the fire. They blackened, and fragments wafted up the chimney. She walked into the spare room across the hall. Crawley's things littered the room. Had he touched everything in her house?

Field met her in the dining room.

~*~

Delany was still shaking when Field reluctantly released her from his arms. She still held his hand as Samuel approached.

"You all right?" Sam asked Delany.

"I've never been so frightened in all my life."

"Philips's men ran off. Freewill is with George. He was beaten pretty badly. Pauline says they were going to hang him."

"Where is Pauline?" Delany asked.

"Outside with George," Sam answered.

"The others?" Field asked.

"Crawley and Philips are tied up in the parlor. Simon has them at gunpoint. They're not going anywhere until the sheriff gets here."

"We better get inside."

Delany hesitated.

Field put his arm around her shoulders and felt her tremble. "I won't leave you."

Together they walked back into the house to await the sheriff.

The magistrate arrived and took Crawley and Philips away.

Delany walked out of the house and into the daylight of the lane.

Field's shadow mingled with her own.

"You were right. I shouldn't have moved here on my own."

"No. You don't have to live in fear. This is your home. It's your right to live here without being assaulted."

"I'm afraid now."

"I will stay with you."

"What do you mean?"

"I mean that until the law changes and we can free the slaves at Archer Hall, I will live here with you."

"We can work to change the law," Delany offered.

"If it never changes, then I'll be content to live here with you. I'll give the hall to my brother."

Delany's heart soared. "Are you sure?"

"Never more sure of anything in my life. I love you, Delany Button Fleet." Field smiled and the warmth that he reserved just for her infused his whole being. "Now will you consent to marry me, please?"

Her spirit answered before she could form the words. It reached for him and entwined. Eyes filled with tears, she choked, "Yes."

He opened his arms.

She stepped into his embrace.

His lips touched hers, and Delany knew she'd arrived home.

Epilogue

One year later

Delany sat on the sofa in the parlor of Button Cove staring at her baby boy while he slept. She'd just changed his nappy, and she was content to watch the little fellow as the sun illuminated the tips of his brown hair to red.

"You're staring at him again." Field sat down next to his wife, who relaxed back into his arms. Contentment such as he'd never experienced filled his heart.

"I just can't help it."

A Devotional Moment

Light is sown for the righteous, and
gladness for the upright in heart. ~ Psalm
97:11

Many of us work for years to get where we
want to be. We do jobs we hate to go up the ladder
to better things. We struggle to bring to fruition all
our goals. Occasionally, we even realize a dream.
But those years of toil can take a toll, and when we
finally reach the top, we may see that while our
material needs have been met, our souls long for
more. God beseeches us to keep pure hearts, to do
what is right for others, and to worship Him with
gladness.

In **The Shopkeeper's Widow**, the protagonist
has worked hard for years and has finally reached
the place she wants to be. However, war has
intervened and may topple everything she's
worked for all her life. When someone comes
forward asking for help, she must decide which is
the most important...her business or the people
who are in great need.

*Have you ever had a sense of uncertainty when
you've finally reached a goal? It's almost as if you*

don't know where to go or what to do. And then, if anything threatens the possession, job, or status in the community, you scramble around trying to figure out how best to hold on to what you have. But it's important to remember that material things, money, status are not important. They can be comforting, but the most important thing is your relationship with God. When you are within God's realm, while human life may not live up to what you expect, when you lean on God you will never be alone. Your soul will rejoice because the Light is always with you. And then, you will own your material belongings, your money and your community status, instead of those things owning you.

LORD, WHEN I AM GIVEN A CHOICE BETWEEN WHAT I MUST DO FOR MYSELF AND WHAT I MUST DO FOR OTHERS, PLEASE GIVE ME THE STRENGTH TO CHOOSE WISELY SO THAT WE ALL MAY PROSPER IN YOU. IN JESUS' NAME I PRAY, AMEN.

Thank you

We appreciate you reading this White Rose Publishing title. For other inspirational stories, please visit our on-line bookstore at www.pelicanbookgroup.com.

For questions or more information, contact us at customer@pelicanbookgroup.com.

White Rose Publishing
Where Faith is the Cornerstone of Love™
an imprint of Pelican Book Group
www.PelicanBookGroup.com

Connect with Us
www.facebook.com/Pelicanbookgroup
www.twitter.com/pelicanbookgrp

To receive news and specials, subscribe to our bulletin
http://pelink.us/bulletin

May God's glory shine through
this inspirational work of fiction.

AMDG

You Can Help!

At Pelican Book Group it is our mission to entertain readers with fiction that uplifts the Gospel. It is our privilege to spend time with you awhile as you read our stories.

We believe you can help us to bring Christ into the lives of people across the globe. And you don't have to open your wallet or even leave your house!

Here are 3 simple things you can do to help us bring illuminating fiction™ to people everywhere.

1) If you enjoyed this book, write a positive review. Post it at online retailers and websites where readers gather. And share your review with us at reviews@pelicanbookgroup.com (this does give us permission to reprint your review in whole or in part.)

2) If you enjoyed this book, recommend it to a friend in person, at a book club or on social media.

3) If you have suggestions on how we can improve or expand our selection, let us know. We value your opinion. Use the contact form on our web site or e-mail us at customer@pelicanbookgroup.com

God Can Help!

Are you in need? The Almighty can do great things for you. Holy is His Name! He has mercy in every generation. He can lift up the lowly and accomplish all things. Reach out today.

Do not fear: I am with you; do not be anxious: I am your God. I will strengthen you, I will help you, I will uphold you with my victorious right hand.

~Isaiah 41:10 (NAB)

We pray daily, and we especially pray for everyone connected to Pelican Book Group—that includes you! If you have a specific need, we welcome the opportunity to pray for you. Share your needs or praise reports at http://pelink.us/pray4us

Free eBook Offer

We're looking for booklovers like you to partner with us! Join our team of influencers today and periodically receive free eBooks!

For more information
Visit http://pelicanbookgroup.com/booklovers

How About Free Audiobooks?

We're looking for audiobook lovers, too! Partner with us as an audiobook lover and periodically receive free audiobooks!

For more information
Visit
http://pelicanbookgroup.com/booklovers/freeaudio.html

or e-mail
booklovers@pelicanbookgroup.com